DELTORA QUEST 2

Cavern of The Fear

DELORA QUEST 2

DELTORA QUEST 2

Cavern of The Fear

Emily Rodda

A Scholastic Press book
from
Scholastic Australia

LEXILE™ 760

Scholastic Press
345 Pacific Highway
Lindfield NSW 2070
an imprint of Scholastic Australia Pty Ltd (ABN 11 000 614 577)
PO Box 579, Gosford NSW 2250.
www.scholastic.com.au

Part of the Scholastic Group
Sydney ● Auckland ● New York ● Toronto ● London ● Mexico City
● New Delhi ● Hong Kong ● Buenos Aires

First published in 2002.
Text and graphics copyright © Emily Rodda, 2002.
Graphics by Bob Ryan.
Cover illustrations copyright © Scholastic Australia, 2002.
Cover illustrations by Marc McBride.

National Library of Australia Cataloguing-in-Publication entry
Rodda, Emily, 1948–.
    Cavern of The Fear.
    ISBN 1 86504 387 7.
    I. Title. (Series: Rodda, Emily, 1948– Deltora quest; 2).
A823.3

Typeset in Palatino.

Printed by McPherson's Printing Group, Maryborough Vic.

10 9 8 7 6 5 4 3 2 1   1 2 3 4 5/0

CONTENTS

1 - Secrets

The flickering lamp made an island of light in the darkness. The wrinkled hand moved slowly across the page.

Outside, the city of Del lay silent, wrapped in sleep. Even those who had long lain awake, grieving for their lost loved ones, had at last fallen into uneasy slumber. The writer's lamp was hidden. The only lights visible in Del burned in the palace on the hill. Lights to comfort the guards who stood watchful by the stairs. Lights that guided two shadows as they slipped through the palace grounds and into the most hidden of its doors.

Soon it would be dawn. But the writer worked on. He had lost all track of time. He had been alone so long that for him day and night had almost lost their meaning.

He ate when he was hungry, and slept when he was tired. And in the long stretches of time between, he wrote, his expert hand rarely faltering, his world shrunk to his secret island of light . . .

The Shadow Lord's tyranny over our land has been ended by the magic and power of the Belt of Deltora. We are free once more, and our king is the same young hero who, with two brave companions, restored the stolen gems to the Belt and brought it home to Del.

The rejoicing of the people can well be imagined. My own rejoicing is no less. But after all I saw in the sixteen years of Shadow Lord rule, and long before that, I am still wary.

The Enemy is defeated but not destroyed. He and the creatures of his sorcery have been driven back across the mountains to the Shadowlands, but I fear he has human servants, too, and they are still among us.

I must therefore remain in hiding until I am certain that the treasure I have protected for so long can be delivered safely to the palace. I try to wait patiently, continuing my work as always, but I confess it is difficult.

Since I have been alone I have been able to make only short visits to the marketplace for news. I dare not stay long away from here. I miss the sun, and have grown very weary of this long, lonely time of waiting.

But the treasure must be guarded. That is the most important thing. There will be time enough for sun and news when the treasure is in King Lief's hands.

I fear I have wandered from my point. This has been happening more and more, of late, and must not continue. My feelings are of no importance. I must restrict myself to my main purpose, which is to paint a word picture of Deltora in this time of tumult.

The Shadow Lord has been banished, but now another battle has begun—a battle against the famine, misery and devastation he has left behind him. Of all the evils facing us, the most terrible is our growing understanding of how many of our people have been taken to the Shadowlands as slaves.

The farms of the north-east and the west have been emptied of people. The best fighters of the Mere and the Plains have been taken. With only one exception, so has every member of the Jalis tribe who was not slaughtered at the time of the invasion. Thousands have gone from Del itself.

The land can be healed and the rivers cleansed. Crops can be sown once more. Houses and workplaces can be repaired. All over Deltora the work has already begun. But the prisoners in the Shadowlands are out of our reach, and their families and friends cannot be comforted.

The marketplace buzzes with talk. There is a growing clamour for a rescue attempt to be made. It has become so loud, of late, that I am sure it is being fermented by Shadow Lord spies. It would suit the Enemy very well for Lief to lead an army across the border. What better way to lay hands on him?

So far, I am thankful to say, Lief has refused even to consider an invasion of the Shadowlands. He must be as aware as I am that without a powerful weapon to combat the Shadow Lord's magic, such an attempt would be a fruitless waste of life.

Yet how his heart must ache when the people cry out to him, and he must deny their hopes.

If only he knew that I could help him! If only he knew I even existed!

They say that he has begun to keep away from crowds, leaving the day-to-day affairs of the kingdom to his mother, Sharn. He spends much of his time alone—shut up, it is said, in the palace library. He shuns even the trusted companions of his quest—Barda, chief of the palace guards, and Jasmine, the wild girl from the Forests of Silence. The only one with whom he spends time is the one-time leader of the Resistance—the stern man all still call Doom.

Perhaps he is searching for some clue as to how he can save the prisoners. Or perhaps he haunts the library because it is safe, and he has realised that he is in constant danger.

Remember, dear Reader: the Belt of Deltora was created by Adin, Deltora's first king, in ancient times. Adin united the seven tribes of Deltora against the Shadow Lord, persuading each tribe to add its talisman, a gem of great power, to the Belt.

And ever since, Adin's heirs by blood have been the only ones for whom the Belt shines.

Lief is Adin's heir. Still little more than a boy himself, he has as yet no child to wear the Belt in his place, should accident or treachery befall him. He has no brother, no sister. His death would lay Deltora open to the Enemy.

Even now, I am certain, the Shadow Lord is hatching plans to lay hands on our land once more. The slaves in the Shadowlands are the bait for one of his traps. But he never relies on just one scheme. A simple plot may succeed where a cunning one fails—and what could be simpler, or quicker, than the thrust of a dagger?

I must not think of these things. I must keep up my spirits, as I pray King Lief is doing. It is vital that he is not driven by frustration to act foolishly. Too much depends on his safety.

I am tired now, and must sleep. The lamp is failing, and my old eyes also. Perhaps I will wake to find that my long wait is over.

I pray that it will be so, for all our sakes. I must show the king what I have to show, before it is too late.

I must tell him, at last, of the Pirran Pipe.

2 - Dangerous Times

As soon as Lief entered his bed chamber, he sensed that danger lurked within it. He glanced down at the Belt of Deltora. Light from the candle he held flickered on the gems set in their medallions of steel.

The rich red of the great ruby, the glowing green of the emerald, had dimmed. The Belt was warning him.

Lief's stomach tightened. He drew his sword. His tired eyes searched the shadows.

He saw nothing. The room looked exactly as it had when he left it that morning. The barred windows were bare, and there was no trailing cover on the bed. Everything that could have concealed an enemy had been removed weeks ago.

Yet there was danger. He knew it.

He moved forward cautiously, ears straining for the slightest sound. The moon, sinking in the sky as dawn approached, cast its light into the room. The shadows of the window bars fell darkly across the bed.

Lief set the candle on the bedside cabinet. He stretched out his hand and, with one sharp movement, stripped the blanket from the bed. The white sheets and pillow gleamed unmarked in the moonlight.

'Show yourself!' he muttered.

Nothing stirred. He looked around the room again, his thoughts raging. What use was a king who was a prisoner of his own fears? Who could not do what his people most wanted him to do?'

He froze as a faint piping sound, a single note, piercingly sweet, filled his mind. The sound lasted for only a brief moment. Then it was gone.

Lief shook his head to clear it. The sound had come to him before. Once in the library, once here in his bed chamber only a week or two ago.

He had mentioned it to no-one. His mother and friends were already worried enough about him. If he had ringing in his ears, it was because he needed rest. And he could not afford to rest. Not until . . .

But he could not hide away from the people for too much longer. The calls for an attempt to rescue the Shadowlands slaves were becoming louder. Soon the people would begin to feel that their hidden king cared nothing for them. Slowly their trust in him would grow less, and at last vanish altogether.

Lief knew this as well as he knew his own name. His own father, kept away from the people, had lost their trust. That was how the gems had been stolen from the

Belt, and the Shadow Lord had triumphed.

He gripped his sword more tightly. It will not happen to me, he told himself. Why else have I been working day and night, but to find a way out of this trap? Tomorrow ...

At the thought of the morrow, he looked longingly at the bed. Perhaps, after all, his nerves had been playing tricks on him.

At that very moment, he heard a tiny scratching, so faint that he was not sure it was real. It seemed to have come from right beside him.

Slowly he slid the point of his sword into the edge of the smooth, white pillow. Gently he tilted the pillow upward.

And there, crouching beneath it, was a Plains scorpion, purple striped with black, and as big as a man's fist. Alerted by the sudden movement, the scorpion reared up, its deadly stinging tail curved to strike.

With a shout, Lief flicked the pillow out of the way. Feathers exploded from its torn side as he smashed the flat of his sword down onto the bed. The scorpion, half-crushed, still struggled to attack. Panting, shuddering with disgust, Lief hammered it again and again, till finally it was still.

The door flew open and Doom, sword in hand, burst into the room. He stopped, staring at the oozing purple mass that stained the white sheet.

Lief sat down heavily on the edge of the bed. Feathers drifted around him, settling on his hair and shoulders. He tried to smile. 'I had a visitor,' he said.

'What is happening?' Jasmine was standing in the doorway. Kree, the black bird who was her constant companion, fluttered behind her. The small furred creature she called Filli blinked sleepily on her shoulder.

Jasmine's green eyes were gleaming as brightly as the dagger in her hand. She moved into the room, taking in the situation at a glance.

'A Plains scorpion,' she said grimly. 'That certainly did not come here of its own accord. But how—?'

'Go back to bed, Jasmine,' Lief broke in. 'I am sorry you were woken. All is well.'

'All is *well*?' exclaimed Jasmine. 'Lief, if you had put your head on that pillow . . .'

Lief shrugged. 'Fortunately, I did not.' He did not say how nearly he had done so.

Jasmine went to the window and tugged at the bars. They came away in her hand.

'The bars have been sawn through, then replaced!' she said. 'So that is how the assassin entered.' She glanced at the sky and her eyes narrowed.

Lief exchanged glances with Doom. They both knew what Jasmine was thinking, now that her first alarm had passed. What had Lief been doing all night, that he should come to his bed chamber for the first time as dawn approached?

'I have been wakeful, but I feel tired now,' Lief said. That, at least, was true, he thought ruefully. He ached for sleep. He pulled the stained sheet from the bed. He would lie on the bare mattress and be glad of it.

'We will leave you in peace, then,' said Doom, moving to the door.

Jasmine knew the words were meant for her. The man they all still called Doom was her father, but over the past weeks he had become as hard to talk to as Lief himself. Every day he was surrounded by people. Every night he disappeared on mysterious business of which Jasmine knew nothing.

He left the room, but Jasmine made no move to follow. This was the first time she had seen Lief alone in weeks. She was determined to speak to him.

But Lief would not look at her. He began to unlace his boots. 'I must have a few hours rest, Jasmine,' he said pointedly. 'We leave for Tora in the morning.'

'*Tora*?' Jasmine stared at him, thunderstruck. 'Lief, you cannot leave Del now! People are clamouring to see you. You *cannot* run away!'

'I do only what I must,' Lief muttered. 'If you choose to think of it as running away, I cannot stop you.'

Filled with unbelieving rage, Jasmine stormed out of the room. She heard the door close behind her, and the key turn in the lock.

The hallway was deserted. Doom had returned to his bed chamber, and no-one else had stirred.

Suddenly Jasmine felt suffocated. She longed for the open air.

She hurried to the great staircase and began to run down, her bare feet making no sound on the cool marble of the floor. If only she had someone to talk to! But she did not.

Barda had taken troops to the city of Noradz, to free the people from their cruel leaders, the Ra-Kacharz, and to collect food for the hungry of Del. Jasmine would have gone with him, but the Noradz people feared Filli, and she could not leave Filli behind. So she had stayed.

Sharn and Doom were always busy. And Lief seemed to have lost all trust in her. He kept secrets he would not share. And now he was running away altogether, to Tora, the great city of the west.

Certainly, he would be safe there. No evil could survive in Tora, which was guarded by its own magic. But surely he did not believe he could hide forever?

Or perhaps he did. Lief had changed. The old Lief, the Lief Jasmine knew, was brave, and eager for action. She was not sure that she liked the new Lief—the secretive, prudent, kingly one—at all.

She reached the ground floor, and the burly guards at the bottom of the stairs moved aside to let her pass. If they thought it odd that she was up so early, they did not say so. In truth, Jasmine thought grimly, they probably expected her to act strangely.

Many tales were told of Jasmine. How she was a fearless fighter who had grown up alone in the dreaded Forests of Silence and could speak to trees and birds. How her mother had died in the Shadowlands. How her father had been injured so badly as to lose his memory, but had escaped to return to Deltora and become Doom, the feared leader of the Resistance.

Uncomfortably aware of the guards' curious eyes upon her, Jasmine threaded her way between the huddled bodies of the hundreds of people who slept on the floor of the vast entrance hall.

The people came seeking help and, above all, hope. All day they waited patiently in line to see Sharn and her helpers. When night came they slept where they had been standing, so as not to lose their places. Many had been there for weeks.

Jasmine moved carefully, hoping that no-one would wake. She dreaded meeting the eyes of those whose loved ones were in the Shadowlands. What could she say to them?

I am sorry. The king says we can do nothing.

The thought of the slaves filled Jasmine with shuddering horror. The loss of freedom was to her worse than death.

With relief she reached the huge entrance doors and slipped outside into the dawn. A lone horseman was approaching the palace at a gallop. As he came closer, Jasmine saw, to her surprise and joy, that it was Barda.

She ran to greet him as he pulled the horse to a halt, but stopped short when she saw the grim lines creasing his tired face.

'Barda, what is wrong?' she exclaimed.

'I bring bad news,' Barda said shortly. 'Noradz is empty. The food has been destroyed. And all the people have been taken—to the Shadowlands.'

3 - Shadows

L ief sat at the great table in the palace kitchens, fighting down rage as he listened to Barda's story. Doom sat opposite him, his face as usual showing no emotion. Beside Doom was Jasmine, her head bowed.

Barda had learned of the Noradz people's fate from Tom, the strange shopkeeper he, Lief and Jasmine had met on their journey through the north.

'When I found the city deserted I went to Tom,' he said. 'I knew he could tell us what had happened, if anyone could. He says the Ra-Kacharz were seen marching the people towards the border. It was only days before the Shadow Lord's defeat.'

Jasmine lifted her head. 'Those people were helpless,' she said bitterly. 'Among them was the girl Tira, who saved our lives. And still we do nothing! We sit here and *talk*! While thousands of souls all over Deltora are willing and able to—'

'Jasmine!' Lief's stomach was churning. 'We cannot

13

march on the Shadowlands. The Shadow Lord's sorcery is too mighty to be defeated on his own ground.'

'But the Belt—' Jasmine began.

'The Belt was made for defence, not attack,' Doom broke in. 'The gems cannot be taken beyond Deltora's borders. Can you have forgotten that, Jasmine? '

Jasmine *had* forgotten it, but she paused for only a moment. 'Then we must invade the Shadowlands without the Belt,' she said stubbornly. 'Deltorans are suffering there in slavery, perhaps in torment—'

'I know this, Jasmine! Not an hour passes that I do not think of it!' cried Lief, jumping to his feet. 'But I cannot send thousands of other Deltorans to their deaths in a hopeless quest to save them. I can do nothing until I find a weapon we can use against the Shadow Lord. I cannot and I *will* not! Do you understand?'

Jasmine's mouth was a thin, hard line. 'I understand only too well, Lief,' she said coldly. 'We are to give the prisoners up for lost, while you go into hiding in Tora. Well, I will have no part of it!'

She turned and almost ran from the room. With a muttered curse, Barda went after her.

Lief slumped back into his chair again. 'She does not understand. Doom, I must tell her—'

'You must *not*!' Doom leaned forward urgently, gripping Lief's arm. 'You must follow the plan in absolute secrecy. It is so important, Lief. It is the *most* important thing. You know it! '

Lief gritted his teeth, then slowly nodded his head.

✦

Meanwhile, Jasmine could no longer hear Barda calling her name. He had gone outside, thinking she would surely make for the open air. She was glad of that. She did not want to be found and soothed. She wanted to stay angry. At least anger was a feeling she understood.

She made her way to the great dining room. She was sure that at this hour it would be deserted.

She was annoyed, therefore, to find that the dining room was not empty at all. Hunched on one side of the huge table was the hulking, savage figure of her old enemy, Glock. Facing him on the other side was the one person she liked even less—Jinks, the malicious little man who had once been a palace acrobat.

Both men were wearing a heavy glove on one hand. Each had a small wooden cage, a mug of ale and a pile of coins at his elbow.

Between them, wrestling on the polished wood, were two huge spiders. One was spotted brown. The other was darker, with a splash of yellow on its back.

At the sound of the opening door, Glock and Jinks turned sharply, but relaxed when they saw who it was.

'Why, it is the king's wild little friend, hero of the quest for the Belt of Deltora,' Jinks jeered. 'To what do we owe the honour of this visit, my lady?'

As he spoke, the spider with the yellow back flipped its opponent over and leaped on top of it, fangs bared.

'Win to Flash?' bawled Glock in excitement.

'Win to Flash!' Jinks agreed resentfully. He pushed

his pile of coins to Glock's side of the table.

Glock snatched up the winning spider in his gloved hand and thrust it into its cage.

The spider which had just escaped death jumped up and threw itself against the cage bars.

'Be still, Fury,' said Jinks, pulling it away none too gently. 'You will have your revenge soon enough.'

'Have you nothing better to do than gamble on fighting spiders?' Jasmine demanded in disgust.

'*You* seem to have nothing better to do than watch us, weakling,' growled Glock. 'Just take yourself off!'

Jinks cleared his throat. 'I hear the king is going to Tora,' he said, his face alight with mischief. 'Are you accompanying him, my lady?'

'No I am not!' snapped Jasmine.

Smiling, Jinks pulled a roll of parchment from his coat and pretended to study it. 'That does not surprise me, under the circumstances,' he murmured.

Jasmine burned to know what he meant, but was determined not to ask.

'Lief should not be going to Tora,' mumbled Glock, filling his mug with ale again. 'He should be raising an army to invade the Shadowlands—making plans to rescue my people!'

'Ah, well, you are the last of the Jalis, my lumbering friend, and the Jalis have always been fools for fighting,' said Jinks, looking down his nose. 'But do you really want to join the rest of your tribe in slavery across the mountains?'

'I would not be captured,' growled Glock. 'I am Glock, the greatest Jalis fighter. I am protected by a powerful talisman, passed down to me by my family through the ages.'

'Oh, indeed!' jeered Jinks.

Glock fumbled under his stained shirt and drew out a small, faded cloth bag which hung on a string around his neck.

'See here!' he shouted, pulling the bag open and tipping a carved lump of wood, three stones, a few tiny twigs and a scrap of shrivelled purple into his enormous hand. 'The talisman of a goblin killed by one of my ancestors. A stone from the belly of a Diamond Serpent, and two more from a dragon's nest. Herbs of great power. And the flower of a Gripper.'

'Oh, I see!' Jinks' small eyes were glittering with amusement. 'So you would be safe in the Shadowlands, would you? You could lead our army to victory?'

'Of course!' said Glock, in a calmer tone, carefully tipping the heap of objects back into the bag. 'And so I have told Lief, again and again. But he will not listen! '

'Ah, he has more important things in mind, just now,' said Jinks, with an all-knowing air.

'You know *nothing* of what is in Lief's mind, Jinks!' flashed Jasmine, very irritated.

Jinks darted a spiteful look in her direction. 'There you are wrong, my lady. I know what I hear.'

'You talk like a fool! And stop calling me "my lady"!' Jasmine exclaimed.

Jinks pursed his lips and went back to studying his parchment.

The silence lengthened, and at last Jasmine's curiosity got the better of her pride. 'Well? What have you heard?' she demanded.

Jinks smiled slyly. 'Why, everyone knows that Lief is going to Tora to find a bride,' he said.

Jasmine felt her face grow hot. 'That is ridiculous!' she cried. 'Lief is far too young to marry.'

Jinks looked her up and down, from her tangled black hair to her bare brown feet.

'Such ignorance is to be expected, no doubt, in one who grew up in a forest, instead of at the palace, as I did,' he said, his lip curling. 'But I had thought you would have known, since you are such a *great* friend of the king's. Why, rumour has it that your own father has been helping him choose the best of the royal jewels for his bride.'

Glock muttered something under his breath and drank deeply, though he had plainly had too much ale already.

'The kings and queens of Deltora always marry young,' Jinks went on, in a lecturing tone. 'It is their duty. Lief must produce an heir as soon as possible—a child to take his place should he die.'

Jasmine did not answer. Of course, what Jinks said made sense. One life was a fragile thing to stand between Deltora and the Shadow Lord. But Lief to marry! Why had he not told her?

Aware of Jinks' sharp eyes upon her, she struggled to keep her face from showing any feeling.

Jinks pushed the parchment towards her. 'See here, if you do not believe me,' he said. 'This is one of the old papers our king has been studying. I made arrangements to . . . ah . . . *borrow* it from the library this morning. I like to keep up with affairs of state.'

'With gossip, you mean,' growled Glock, burying his nose in his ale once more.

Jasmine glanced at the parchment. It was covered in names, lines and symbols. At the top was a title in flowing script.

The Great Families of Tora

'You see?' crowed Jinks. 'Lief will choose his queen from one of the *best* Toran families.'

Glock snorted. 'Why go all the way to Tora for a wife? he slurred. 'There are plenty of pretty girls in Del.'

Jinks looked at him with disdain. 'Lief is following ancient ways,' he said loftily. 'Adin himself married a Toran, and his children did the same. Adin was a wily bird. He knew the value of keeping strong links between east and west.'

'The Torans say that Adin married for love,' retorted Jasmine.

Jinks sniggered knowingly. 'No doubt the Toran lady in question was high-born, well-read and very beautiful,' he said. 'I daresay Adin was pleased enough with his choice. As Lief will be in his turn.'

Glock guffawed into his mug, spattering the table with specks of foam.

Jasmine could not bear their company any more. She left the room and made for the kitchen.

But before she could reach it, she was stopped by the sound of Sharn's voice.

'Jasmine! Barda was looking for you,' Sharn called, hastening towards her. 'Now he has gone to his rest, for he rode all night. And Lief and Doom said to say goodbye. They have just left for Tora.'

Seeing Jasmine's frown, and misunderstanding it, Sharn smiled kindly. 'They will be quite safe, Jasmine. Toran magic will speed their journey. They may have arrived even now. They will be back in a day or two.'

'Bringing someone with them, I believe,' Jasmine answered in a hard voice. 'A young lady, of high birth.'

Sharn's eyes widened. 'Who told you that?' she asked sharply.

Jasmine shrugged. 'I cannot remember now,' she lied. 'It is true, though, I imagine?'

Sharn hesitated. 'I can tell you nothing,' she said at last. 'I am sorry.'

That was answer enough for Jasmine. She gave a small nod, and turned to go.

Sharn bit her lip. 'Do not be angry with Lief, Jasmine,' she pleaded. 'He is only doing what he must— what is his duty.'

'Oh, I understand,' said Jasmine coolly. 'I understand completely.'

4 -By Order of the King

B y the time Jasmine reached the great stairway, she had made up her mind. She could stay in the palace no longer.

'We will go back to the Forests where we belong,' she murmured to Filli and Kree. 'I am tired of palaces, and rules—and kings.'

There was a tightness in her chest and a dull ache in the pit of her stomach as she began to climb the stairs.

Something stopped her and she looked down to see a thick silver rope strung across the stairway. She had been so lost in thought that she had gone past the second floor where the bed chambers were.

Ahead was the library floor—forbidden to all except Lief, Doom and Sharn.

The very sight of the rope barrier annoyed Jasmine. On a sudden, defiant impulse, she crawled under it. If Jinks could disobey the rule, then so could she

At the top of the stairs was a large, square space.

21

Two huge palace guards sat against the far wall. Half-finished mugs of ale stood on a table between them.

Jasmine half-turned, ready to retreat. But the men did not move or speak. They were asleep.

Jasmine smiled wryly. No doubt the ale was a gift from Jinks. This was how he had 'arranged' to steal Lief's parchment.

She looked around. To her left was a high, arched door marked 'LIBRARY'. But to her right, a broad hallway led towards the back of the palace. It was barred by yet another silver rope.

So this floor held more secrets than the library. What secrets?

Kree fluttered anxiously as Jasmine crept past the guards, ducked under the rope and moved swiftly into the dimness of the hallway. He had never trusted this shadowy palace, where trees did not grow and the sky could be seen only through windows. And here he felt especially uneasy.

At first, Jasmine found the hallway disappointing. There were storerooms on the right-hand side. All were filled with books and papers except the last, which was blackened and empty. There had plainly been a fire there long ago.

That was no loss, I am sure, Jasmine thought bitterly. *There are more than enough old books in this place.*

The wall on her left seemed totally blank. But at the very end, she found something strange.

An archway opened onto a short corridor. But the

corridor ended in a wall of roughly-laid bricks, upon which there was a notice. Jasmine felt a strange tingle of excitement. She ran to the wall and slowly spelled out the words on the notice.

SEALED BY ORDER OF THE KING

So. Here was another of Lief's kingly secrets.

Obeying an urge she could not explain, Jasmine pressed her ear against the bricks.

Thump! Thump!

The sound was coming from the other side of the wall! Jasmine closed her eyes, listening intently.

The muffled throbbing grew stronger, stronger, pounding like a great heartbeat. The rough bricks grew warm under Jasmine's cheek. The sound filled her mind, vibrated through her body.

Thump! Thump! Thump!

The notice fell down. Tiny pieces of mortar began dropping from between the bricks, pattering to the floor like hailstones. The bricks grew hotter, hotter . . .

Suddenly, Jasmine's need to reach the source of the sound became overwhelming. Forgetting all about the sleeping guards and the need for silence, she beat the wall with her fists.

The bricks seemed to tremble. Mortar showered from between them, falling onto Jasmine's feet.

Kree clucked warningly. Filli squeaked in fright.

'It is all right,' Jasmine soothed. But she was

trembling as she pulled out her dagger and began to scrape more of the crumbling mortar away.

Thump! Thump! Thump!

The bricks shuddered, moving in their places with harsh, clinking sounds. Jasmine staggered back as one came free and fell to the floor. Behind the hole it had left was a heavy brass doorknob.

Lief and the Belt have gone. Now is our chance. Come to me . . .

The thought was clear, so clear. Like a voice. The summons was urgent. It could not be denied.

More mortar was falling by the moment. Jasmine put away her dagger and began tearing at the bricks, pulling out one, then another. Now she could see the deeply carved wood that surrounded the doorknob. The gap in the wall was just big enough for her to crawl through.

Come to me . . .

Jasmine twisted the doorknob. The door swung smoothly open. Ignoring Kree's warning cry, she squeezed through the hole into the room beyond.

When she was inside, she stood, staring.

What was this place? It was quite different from anything else she had seen in the palace. The walls were smooth, white and gleaming, and so was the floor. There were no windows, yet there was light—harsh, white light that hurt her eyes.

Suddenly she knew without question that she should not be here. Filli whimpered. Kree shrieked a warning from the hallway. Jasmine spun around, but already the door was closing behind her. Before she could reach it, it had shut with a small, final click.

Thump! Thump!

Jasmine froze. The sound was deep, throbbing and loud—so loud it drowned out every thought. Slowly she turned away from the door.

The sound was coming from the centre of the room. From something that was shrouded in a heavy black cloth. Drawn by a force she had no will to resist, Jasmine stumbled towards the black shape, stretched out her hand, and pulled the cloth away.

Thump! Thump! Thump!

Underneath the cloth was a small table. Its surface was thick, curved glass, rippling like water. Jasmine stared. The sound filled her body and her mind. The moving surface seemed to draw her. She bent over it, staring into its transparent depths.

Slowly the throbbing sound died away. The ripples began to swirl and colour, becoming grey as smoke with rims of red. In the centre of the ripples was a core of darkness.

'Jasmine! It is you!'

The voice drifted from the swirling darkness—young, sweet and warm.

Jasmine caught her breath. 'Who are you?' she whispered. 'How do you know my name?'

'I knew you would hear me, Jasmine,' sighed the voice. 'I called and called.'

'Who are you? *Where* are you?' Jasmine bent low over the table, straining to see beyond the darkness.

'Where I was born,' sighed the voice. 'The other slaves grieve for Deltora, but I have known no home but this.'

Jasmine gripped the edge of the table to steady herself. 'The Shadowlands,' she murmured.

'Yes,' whispered the voice. 'Yes, of course, but I must make haste. If I am discovered using the crystal . . . '

There was a choking sob. Then the voice began again, though more unsteadily than before.

'I must not cry. I must be brave, as you are, Jasmine. Our mother told me that. She said that in the Forests you feared nothing. You—'

Jasmine's heart seemed to stop. '*What* did you say?' she breathed. '*Our mother?*'

The young voice ran on, the words tumbling over one another.

'Mother said you would help us. Before she died, she told me. She said that I must somehow reach the crystal, and call you. She said I would know when it was time. And I did, Jasmine! I did!'

Jasmine was panting as though she had been running. 'How did you know?' she whispered.

'Red clouds swirled back over the mountains. There was thunder, and terrible anger. The creatures moaned and gnashed their teeth.'

'Wait . . .' Jasmine begged wildly. 'Tell me—'

But the voice was excited now. 'I knew what the

anger meant. You defeated the Shadow Lord, didn't you, Jasmine? You—and the other, the son of our father's friend. The one who will not listen to me. Who sealed away the crystal, so you could not hear me . . .'

'Lief,' said Jasmine through lips that were stiff, and hard to move.

'Yes. He does not want you to know me. He fears the Shadow Lord. But I did not give up hope. Mother said you would not know you had a sister, for I was just beginning when she was taken from the Forests, but I should tell you . . .'

Jasmine tore herself away from the table, her head reeling. She could not take this in.

'Jasmine, are you still there?' The young voice was suddenly sharp with panic.

Jasmine took a deep, shuddering breath. She leaned forward and looked into the swirling, smoky surface of the table once more.

She concentrated—searching, searching—and then, deep in the black core, she saw a face—a girl child's face, surrounded by a tangled mass of black hair. Pointed chin, wide, frightened green eyes . . . It was like looking in a mirror, but a mirror that reflected her own image as it was years ago.

'I am here,' Jasmine said huskily.

'You must hurry,' the girl whispered. 'We are to be put to death, all of us, very soon. The Shadow Lord has decreed it. It is revenge for what you and the ones called Lief and Barda did to him. Please—oh!'

The image in the blackness wavered and faded
'I must go,' the voice said rapidly. 'I hear them.'
'Wait! What is your name?' Jasmine called.
'Faith. My name is Faith.' The voice was very faint
now. The image had disappeared, overcome by swirling
greyness, which was itself fading away.
'I will find you, Faith!' Jasmine shouted desperately.
'Do not despair! I will find you!'

✦

Jasmine was still shaking as she ran down the stairs to
the ground floor and began pushing through the crowd.
People stared as she passed. Some called to her, but
she did not hear. A dark, clever-faced man caught her
arm. She shook off his hand, and hurried on.
She reached the doors and saw that the crowd had
spilled onto the steps and down into the garden. She
ran towards the gates and out into the road beyond.
She had to find a peaceful place where she could
think clearly. But where could she go?
Then an idea came to her. Lief's old home—the
blacksmith's forge! It was not far from the palace, and it
would offer the peace she needed.
She set off, moving swiftly through the long grass
at the side of the road. Her shocked mind was seething
with wild plans. So it was that she did not hear the
furtive footsteps behind her, or feel the eyes of the one
who was following.

5 - Meetings

In a beautiful, light-filled room in the marble city of Tora, Lief took the hand of the gentle young woman whose great dark eyes were fixed on his own. There were three other people in the room, but Lief spoke to the girl as though they were alone.

'You are willing, Marilen?' he asked softly.

Half eager, half afraid, the girl glanced up at a tall man whose hand rested protectively on her shoulder. She looked so like him that he could only be her father.

The man hesitated. 'Toran magic will not protect Marilen so far away in Del,' he said at last. 'She is my only child, and very precious to me.'

Doom, who had been standing behind Lief, stepped forward. 'Marilen is precious to the whole of Deltora now,' he said firmly. 'She will be well guarded.'

'Whatever I have will be hers,' added Lief, more quietly. 'And my mother will treat her as her own.'

The man bowed his head. 'Her own mother would

have been very proud, this day,' he murmured.

Marilen turned back to Lief. 'I am willing,' she said. 'It is a great honour. I will try to be worthy.'

'You will not have to try, Marilen.' A grey-haired woman moved to the girl's side.

It was Zeean, the Toran leader who had nearly lost her life in the final conflict with the Shadow Lord in Del. Her scarlet robe shone like a jewel in the sunlight reflecting from the white walls of the room.

'This day will do much to undo the evils of the past,' she said.

She gestured at the scrolls of parchment scattered on a nearby table. 'It is not the way of Torans to keep old writings. We left that to the librarians of Del. A mistake, perhaps. But we will study these carefully now.'

'Indeed,' agreed Marilen's father fervently.

'Thank you,' said Lief. 'And there is something more that—'

'Perhaps we should leave Marilen to prepare for her journey?' Doom interrupted smoothly.

Zeean smiled. Bowing to Marilen and her father, she led the way out of the house, and into a vine-hung courtyard where a sparkling fountain played.

'And so, Lief?' she asked, when she had settled herself by the fountain's edge. 'What did you want to ask me, that even Marilen must not know?'

Lief leaned forward. 'The prisoners in the Shadowlands, Zeean. Is there a chance—any at all—that Toran magic could help us set them free?'

Zeean's brow creased as she shook her head. 'I am sorry. Our power within Tora is great, but outside our boundaries it is very limited. It could not aid you in a quest to the Shadowlands.'

She sighed as Lief's face fell. 'I fear you must accept that there is nothing that would do so, Lief. According to legend, the only thing the Shadow Lord ever feared in his own domain was the music of the Pirran Pipe.'

Lief's mind was suddenly pierced with sound. A single, piping note, almost unbearably sweet. Tears sprang into his eyes. He gaped at Zeean, unable to move, unable to speak.

The sound died away, and he became aware that Doom was shaking his arm and calling his name.

'I am all right,' he managed to say. He blinked at Zeean. 'This—Pirran Pipe. Tell me . . .'

'The Pipe's magic was a thing of legend, not truth, I think, and I know little of it,' the old woman said, her face troubled.

'Still—tell me, please!' begged Lief.

Zeean glanced at Doom, then nodded uncertainly. 'The Pirran Pipe is—or was—a flute, or pipe, of great magic and power. It is said to have existed in the lands beyond the mountains long, long ago. Before they became the Shadowlands.'

'So—this Pirran Pipe existed *before* the rise of the Shadow Lord?' Doom asked.

'Indeed. I heard of it as a child. From a Jalis traveller I met by the river. It was part of a tale he told me as he caught fish for his dinner. But what the tale was . . .' Zeean thought carefully, but finally shook her head.

'I am sorry. It was so long ago. I remember only what I have told you, and the strange, rough looks and speech of the man. Also, that he said—' She smiled. 'He said that the tale was first told to a girl child of my own years, by a black bird.'

'Then it was one of the Tenna Birdsong Tales!' exclaimed Doom. 'Ancient Jalis folk stories. I have heard Glock speak of them.'

'I would not have thought Glock a very reliable source of information,' Zeean said dryly. 'But if these Birdsong stories are of the Jalis, you can soon find out about the Pirran Pipe. The folk tales of all the seven tribes are in the first volume of *The Deltora Annals*. Adin insisted that—'

She broke off as Lief groaned with frustration. 'What is wrong?' she asked.

'All the volumes of *The Deltora Annals* were burned in the time of King Alton, my grandfather,' said Lief flatly.

'*Burned*? Zeean's face, usually so calm, filled with startled horror. 'But the *Annals* contained Deltora's oldest history! It was the only record—'

'Indeed,' said Lief. 'But it was burned, nonetheless, on the orders of King Alton's chief advisor, Prandine.' His face twisted as he spoke the hated name. 'The palace librarian who was forced to carry out the order was a man called Josef. He threw himself on the flames, rather than live with the knowledge of what he had done.'

'Terrible!' Zeean breathed. 'Why burn the *Annals*?'

'Because a land which does not remember its history can never learn the lessons of its past,' said Doom soberly. 'I fancy those old books contained things the Shadow Lord wanted forgotten. Among them, perhaps, the Tenna Birdsong Tales. One in particular . . .'

Lief looked up quickly. 'The tale of the Pirran Pipe?'

'Why not? There are those who claim that many of the old folk tales are based on truth,' said Doom. His lean, sun-browned face was taut with excitement.

'You cannot surely have it in your minds to try to find the Pirran Pipe?' Zeean shook her head in disbelief. 'Why, that is madness. If the Pipe ever existed at all, it surely exists no longer. Its country has become the Shadowlands! And, whatever the Shadow Lord feared, it did not defeat him.'

'We do not yet know the whole story,' said Lief. 'There may have been a reason—'

'Indeed,' Doom broke in. 'We must return to Del with all speed, as soon as Marilen can be ready. We must speak to Glock. He may not be the most reliable storyteller we could find, but he is the only Jalis left alive in Deltora. The only one who might be able to tell us what we need to know.'

＋

Far away, at the forge in Del, morning shadows still lay across the cottage and the overgrown herb garden.

Jasmine felt her tight muscles beginning to relax as

the peace of the place enfolded her.

When he first became king, Lief had declared that he would not live in the palace, but would go back to the forge, where he had spent his childhood.

But the move had been delayed, and delayed again. And now—well, now Lief was to take a Toran bride, so of course it would never happen.

Jasmine had seen the marble, fountains and fine things of Tora. She could not imagine a lady from that place living in a humble dwelling.

So the move to the forge had all been a dream and a lie. As her faith in Lief had been.

She stared sightlessly at the peeling paint of the cottage door. Because Lief was determined not to invade the Shadowlands, he had decided that she must never know about her sister. So he had sealed the room. How had he *dared* to make such a decision?

No wonder he has been avoiding me, Jasmine thought. No wonder he cannot meet my eyes.

By Order of the King . . .

Feeling her anger rise again, she turned her back on the cottage and walked across the yard to the forge itself.

She peered into the place where the great fire had once burned. The heavy hammers, tongs and bellows lay close at hand, as though waiting for their owners to return. It was strange to think that Lief had once worked here, helping his father to make horseshoes and plough shares for the people of the city.

But something else was strange, too, and at last Jasmine saw it.

The forge had lain idle for almost a year. The tools should have been covered with dust. But they were not. And—was it her imagination, or did the metal of the forge seem warmer than it should?

Jasmine looked around. An old chair stood nearby. Its back was dusty, but the seat was partly clean, as though, perhaps, a jacket or cloak had been thrown over it not so long ago.

And on the ground behind one of the chair legs was a folded scrap of paper. It showed no sign of the yellowing of age. So it had been dropped recently. Probably it had slipped from the pocket of the garment that had been thrown over the chair.

Jasmine picked up the paper and unfolded it.

EPPN—GPSHF 22 UPOJHIY —M

The letters and figures made no sense at all to Jasmine. But she was sure of one thing: Lief had written the note. She had seen his writing too often to be mistaken. This was some sort of code. Yet another secret.

She threw the note to the ground in irritation.

'It seems you are displeased,' said an amused voice behind her.

6 - Treasure

Snatching her dagger from her belt, Jasmine spun around. A man was standing watching her. It was the dark, clever-faced man who had tried to talk to her in the entrance hall of the palace. He must have moved as silently as a cat, Jasmine thought, for neither she nor Kree had heard him approach.

The man smiled, white teeth flashing against his brown skin.

The smile made him look younger than Jasmine had first thought. In fact, it was hard to tell what age he might be. His body was lean, but strong. His face was unlined. His hazel eyes were clear and amused. His straight black hair was long, and tied back in a band.

He took a step towards her.

'Keep back,' Jasmine muttered warningly, holding her dagger so that it flashed in a shaft of sunlight.

The man stopped, and held his arms away from his body to show that he held no weapon.'I mean you no harm,' he said, without the slightest sign of fear. 'I have a favour to ask of you.'

'Speak, then,' said Jasmine, admiring his coolness in spite of herself.

'I have a friend who has something of great value to give the king,' said the man. 'I have been waiting in the palace on his behalf for many days now. I followed you in the hope that you would help us.'

Jasmine laughed bitterly. 'If you think I have influence with Lief, you are very much mistaken,' she said. 'You would do better to go back to the palace and stand in line again.'

The man raised one eyebrow. 'I have had enough of standing in line,' he said.

Jasmine nodded slowly. She recognised in this man a fellow spirit. Someone who disliked rules, and who went his own way. But the last thing she needed now was to become entangled in another problem connected with the palace. She had to plan, to prepare . . .

'Let me take you to see my friend, I beg you,' the man said. 'The treasure he has been guarding is priceless. Believe me, the king will be grateful.'

Jasmine had no wish to earn Lief's gratitude. She wanted never to see him again. Yet . . . if this man was speaking the truth, and his friend's treasure was indeed valuable, it would cause a great sensation in the palace.

And a sensation was what she needed. She was too well-known to travel all the way to the Shadowlands border without being recognised. If Sharn heard of what she was doing, she would try to stop her. But if Sharn's attention was diverted, even for a day or two . . .

'What is this treasure?' she asked abruptly.

The stranger shook his head. 'That is for my friend to tell,' he said. 'He has suffered much to guard it.'

Jasmine watched him narrowly. Could he be trying to lure her into a trap?

'You have no reason to trust me,' the man said, as if reading her mind. 'I do not ask you to do so. Walk behind me with your dagger in my back, if you wish.'

Jasmine made her decision. She nodded briskly. 'Lead on, then,' she said. 'But I warn you. One false move, and I will not hesitate to kill you. And whatever this treasure is, it had better be worth my while!'

✦

As the stranger led her into the heart of Del, Jasmine told herself that she had been right to trust him. When, however, he stopped at the burned-out shell of an old pottery, she shook her head.

'Do you really expect me to enter that place with you?' she exclaimed. 'I am not so foolish.'

The man sighed. 'No doubt you have good reason to be suspicious. But I am the last person likely to be a threat to your safety. Fighting and weapons do not appeal to me in the slightest. My friend lives within.'

'Tell him to bring the treasure out to me,' Jasmine ordered abruptly.

'He will not do that,' said her companion. 'He does not believe Del is safe.'

Tired of the argument, Kree squawked loudly, left Jasmine's shoulder and flew into the air.

Jasmine nodded. 'Kree will follow you,' she said. 'I will wait until he brings me word that all is safe.'

The man looked up at the circling bird, and gave a low whistle. 'So the stories are true,' he murmured. 'You *do* talk to birds.'

Jasmine did not answer. The man shrugged and climbed through a gap in the ruined wall. Kree soared after him. Soon both of them had vanished from view.

Minutes crawled by. Suddenly nervous, Jasmine looked behind her, but the street was deserted.

Then she heard a harsh cry and saw a black streak racing towards her, dark against the sky.

Filli chattered excitedly and scurried out from under Jasmine's collar. 'Yes, Filli, it seems that we are to discover treasure after all,' Jasmine said. Despite everything, she felt a small thrill of excitement.

She climbed into the pottery, and began picking her way through the blackened rubble inside.

The stranger was waiting for her beside a gaping hole in the floor near the back of the building. With him, sitting on a large chest made of woven cane, was a frail, white-haired old man. Seeing Jasmine approach, the old man struggled to his feet.

When she reached him, and he was able to see her clearly, he looked rather surprised.

'Are you *sure* this is a lady of the palace, my boy?' he asked, in a piercing whisper.

His companion smiled. 'There is nothing more certain,' he said. 'This is Jasmine, who helped King Lief restore the Belt of Deltora. We are greatly honoured by her presence.'

Jasmine squirmed, and darted him a furious look. His smile did not waver.

The old man nodded gently. 'Of course, times have changed,' he murmured. 'We do not have the leisure for plaited hair, fine clothes and trinkets now. So much the better, perhaps.'

With great dignity, he bowed low to Jasmine. 'Thank you for agreeing to see me, madame,' he said. 'I have come out to greet you, for I fear the steps of our home are very steep.'

He waved his hand at the hole in the floor, and Jasmine realised that it was in fact a trapdoor that led down to a deep cellar.

She had hardly taken this in when the old man was speaking again. 'I have waited long for this moment,' he said. 'May I present myself? I am Josef, once Palace Librarian to King Alton. I—I wish to give you these.'

His hand trembled as he lifted the lid of the chest on which he had been sitting.

Jasmine looked down, and her heart sank. She had thought of many things the treasure might be. But she had not thought of this!

The chest was filled to the brim with old books, all bound in the same pale blue cloth, all the same size, and all with exactly the same gold lettering on the front.

The Deltora Annals

She raised her head to look at Josef once more. He had drawn himself up, plainly waiting for a reaction.

'*The Deltora Annals*?' she repeated stupidly.

A smile transfigured the old man's wrinkled face, making it glow. 'Of course you are shocked,' he said gleefully. 'You believed the *Annals* to have been burned in their storeroom, many years ago. And I with them. But I played a little trick on Prandine, you see. Yes, so I did.'

He laughed. 'I could not disobey his order openly. But neither could I bear to burn Deltora's history. So I set a fire in the storeroom, and left a note saying I had put an end to myself. Then I, and the *Annals,* escaped the palace to hide and wait for happier times.'

His eyes were sparkling. 'And we survived, as you see—of later years with the help of Ranesh, my apprentice, who brought you here. Is it not wonderful? Will not the young king rejoice?'

Jasmine forced a smile, and nodded. She did not want to disappoint the courteous, excited old man. She would help him and Ranesh take the old history books to the palace.

But she was sure, absolutely positive, that no-one would care about them at all. Least of all Lief.

7 - Doran the Dragonlover

Jasmine had often said that she would never understand the ways of the palace. She was even more sure of it when she saw how Josef was greeted.

On seeing what was in the cane chest, Sharn shrieked with amazement and delight. And she was not the only one. In moments the great entrance hall was ringing with the voices of people cheering.

Jasmine stood silently by, shaking her head in bewilderment, waiting for her chance to slip away.

'Thank you for helping us,' a voice said in her ear. The man she now knew as Ranesh was beside her.

'It was nothing,' Jasmine said, shrugging.

'You did not realise the importance of the *Annals*, did you?' Ranesh persisted. 'I saw it in your face when Josef opened the chest.'

'Old books are not what I think of as treasure, certainly,' Jasmine answered shortly.

Ranesh laughed. 'When I met Josef, years ago, I

would have agreed with you. I was just a ragged orphan, then—living by thieving in the streets of Del. I thought Josef was an old fool to have given up life in the palace for the sake of a few old books. Now—I feel differently.'

His sharp hazel eyes softened as they looked at the old man bowing to the admirers crowding around him.

'It is good to see Josef receiving the honour he deserves,' he murmured. 'I owe him much. He taught me to read and write. He gave me a home. He taught me to live without stealing—well, almost!'

His white teeth flashed in another smile. 'After the pottery was raided by the Grey Guards, and the kind people who had fed us were taken, we were often very hungry. Occasionally, I admit, I persuaded myself that what Josef did not know would not hurt him, and went back to my old ways to feed us both.'

'You were lucky to survive the raid yourselves,' said Jasmine.

Ranesh's smile disappeared. 'The Grey Guards did not find the cellar, and the fire did not touch it either. It grew warm, though. For a time I thought Josef and I would be roasted like ducks in an oven—and *The Deltora Annals* with us.'

'Would it really have mattered?' Jasmine sighed. 'About the books, I mean,' she added hastily, as the man raised an eyebrow.

'I think so,' he said. 'They are not just dry history, you know, but a day-by-day account of events in the kingdom for many centuries. Every volume is full of tales, sketches, maps—'

'*Maps*?' Jasmine asked, suddenly alert.

'Of course,' said Ranesh, glancing at her curiously. 'Are you interested in maps?'

'If they show me how to reach places I want to go,' said Jasmine cautiously. 'And if I can understand them.'

Ranesh grinned. 'Then you should look at my favourites, in volume 5. They are only rough sketches, but I would trust them with my life. They were made by Doran the Dragonlover.'

He looked at Jasmine to see if the name meant anything to her, and, seeing that it did not, went on:

'Doran was a famous traveller who explored Deltora from the coasts to the Shadowlands border. He always wrote in the *Annals* with his own hand. He said he could not trust the librarians to do it, for they introduced errors by making his words too polite and his map lines too neat. Doran was a great character, and a man of many talents, who . . .'

Jasmine was no longer listening. She had begun to think rapidly, calculating the best way of gaining some time alone with the *Annals*. Doran's maps sounded just what she needed, if she was to find the fastest, most secret way to the Shadowlands.

'Jasmine?' It was Sharn's voice. Jasmine looked up.

'Jasmine, would you be so kind as to take the *Annals* to the library and stay with them for a time?' Sharn asked quietly. 'I would like Josef and Ranesh to take some refreshment, but Josef will not rest until the books are safe, under the eye of someone he trusts.'

Rather startled that her wish had been granted so immediately, Jasmine agreed willingly. In moments she was running up the stairs while a palace guard followed, carrying the chest of books.

Sharn took Josef and Ranesh into the kitchen where a meal had been prepared for them. She returned to her duties with a far lighter heart than she had begun them that morning. How overjoyed Lief would be to hear of the unexpected return of the *Annals*!

It was also wonderful to see Jasmine happy. The girl seemed relieved, for a time at least, of her misery over the fate of the prisoners in the Shadowlands.

And that means, Sharn thought gratefully, that *I* can be relieved, for a time at least, of the fear that she will do something foolish.

✦

As soon as the palace guard had put down the chest and left the library, Jasmine searched rapidly through the *Annals* until she found the one marked '5'.

As she picked it up, it fell open at a page with no ruled lines, and covered in untidy printing. Jasmine guessed it had been opened at this place many times before. The page was signed 'Doran'.

Doran the Dragonlover might have been a man of many talents, Jasmine thought, but he had plainly not valued neatness. He had scribbled down his report, and a verse, then corrected them both at a later date, using a different pen and darker ink.

My recent journey to the Os-Mine Hills was disastrous. I went there hoping to find a dragon's lair, having read the Tenna Birdsong ~~tale~~ legend 'The Girl With the Golden Hair' in volume 1 of the Annals. My foolish ~~quest~~ resulted only in a bloody nose, a sore head and a shivering fever caused by sleeping the night through while soaked to the skin.

I have no memory of what brought these calamities about. I cannot have fallen foul of a dragon, for I still live. I cannot have met with a granous, for I still possess all my fingers and toes. No doubt I merely slipped and fell into some foul stream, cracking my stupid skull.

The rhyme below was spinning in my head when I awoke from my daze. It is clearly ~~may offer some clue or be merely~~ the product of a rattled brain. ~~I must find out.~~

SONG OF THE DEAD

'Above our ~~land~~ heads the tumult rages
Struggle echoes through the ages
There the strife will never cease
But here below we ~~dwell~~ rest in peace
Where ~~timeless tides~~ tides of time swamp memory
Our sunless prison makes us free.
The gem-glow lights our ~~rocky~~ earthy walls
And dragons guard our shining halls.'

NOTE: I AM NOW CONVINCED THAT THE OS-MINE HILLS ARE HIGHLY DANGEROUS & OF NO INTEREST TO THE TRAVELLER.

DORAN

46

Tears were burning in Jasmine's eyes as she read the last words of the verse and thought of her mother, dead in the Shadowlands. Yet . . . it seemed to her that something about the rhyme did not quite ring true.

Frowning, she read the whole page again. The more she looked at Doran's hasty corrections and added lines, the more she became convinced that they were intended to conceal something. Curiosity buzzed in her mind like an annoying insect.

Quickly she sorted through the books she had unloaded on the library table, searching for Volume 1.

+

An hour later, Josef came hobbling into the library, leaning on Ranesh's arm and exclaiming with delight on seeing his old place of work once more.

He was delighted to see Jasmine sitting at a table on which several volumes of the *Deltora Annals* lay scattered. One volume was open in front of her, and she had plainly been taking notes from it.

'Can I help you, my dear?' he asked, hurrying forward.

'Thank you, but it is not necessary,' said Jasmine, hastily closing the book and stuffing the paper on which she had been writing into her pocket.

She pushed her chair back, and stood up. 'I must leave you,' she said. 'There are things I must do.'

'Why, of course!' exclaimed Josef, patting her arm. 'You run along. Ranesh and I have much to do also. We have been asked to stay in the palace, to care for the

Annals and the other books! Is it not wonderful?'

'Indeed it is,' said Jasmine warmly. She was very glad that the old man's devotion had been rewarded. Besides, she owed him much. She could hardly contain her excitement as she thought of the paper she had in her jacket pocket.

She hurried to the door, then turned back. She was almost certain that she was right in what she had worked out, but it was best to be quite sure.

'Josef,' she said, as casually as she could. 'If *Annals* writers changed their minds about what they had written, were they permitted to tear out the page?'

Josef looked shocked. 'Oh, certainly not!' he said. 'Small *corrections* could be made, under supervision. But that was all. Why do you ask?'

'Oh, no particular reason,' Jasmine answered carelessly, but her heart was racing as she left the library. Nodding brightly to the guards who had replaced the ones she had crept by that morning, she ran down the stairs to her bed chamber.

It was a matter of moments to pack her belongings. The vine growing on the wall outside her window was sturdy. It supported her easily as she swung herself out and began to climb down.

She had almost reached the ground when Kree squawked a warning. Jasmine looked down and groaned. Glock was standing below, glaring up at her.

'What do you think you are doing, Miss?' he growled.

8 - Discoveries

It was deepest night when Lief and Doom returned to Del with Marilen. Like thieves, the three slipped into the silent palace by the kitchen door.

Sharn was sitting at the table, waiting for them. She jumped up, her face wreathed in relieved smiles.

'You are really here!' she cried. 'When your message came that you would be back so soon, I could hardly believe it.'

She hastened to settle Marilen by the stove with a mug of hot soup. Then she drew Lief aside. 'I have much to tell you!' she whispered. 'There is wonderful news, but bad news as well.'

Doom's voice interrupted them. 'I am going to wake Glock,' he called from the door. 'We should talk to him at once.'

'Why *Glock*?' Sharn demanded. 'What has he to do with—'

'I will tell you later, Mother,' Lief said in a low voice,

as Doom left the room. 'Give me your news. The bad news first, while we cannot be overheard.'

He nodded towards Marilen, who was leaning towards the stove, warming her chilled hands. The girl looked delicate, defenceless and very tired. If she was frightened on her first night at the palace, she might beg to return to Tora. Such a request could not be denied, so it was vital that it was never made.

'Guards reporting for duty on the third floor this afternoon found that the two men they were to replace were asleep, and would not wake,' Sharn whispered. 'We believe they were given a powerful sleeping potion in some ale.'

Lief felt the chill that always came over him when he thought of the third floor. 'The sealed room!' he whispered. 'Had the wall been—?'

Sharn nodded reluctantly, seeing lines of worry deepen on her son's face. 'The mortar between the bricks had crumbled away, and some of the bricks had fallen. But the hole was small, and the door beyond was shut fast. Perhaps the intruder was disturbed before he could enter.'

'We must just hope that is so,' Lief muttered. 'Has the damage been repaired?'

'Of course,' his mother answered.

She glanced at the drooping figure of the girl in the armchair. 'Poor child. What a place she has come to! And she is so young . . .'

Lief smiled ruefully. 'No younger than me,' he

reminded her. 'Or Jasmine.'

'Oh!' Sharn exclaimed. 'That reminds me! The good news! *The Deltora Annals* has been returned to us. And it was Jasmine who brought it about.'

She had expected her son to be pleased. But even she was startled at the sudden, disbelieving joy that lit his face. Before she could ask him to explain it, however, Doom strode back into the kitchen, his face like thunder.

'Glock is not in his bed!' he muttered. 'No doubt he is snoring under a table in some tavern in the city.'

'Let him snore!' Lief grinned. 'We do not need him any longer!'

✦

Soon afterwards, Lief and Doom were being excitedly welcomed by Josef. His white hair ruffled, the folds of his borrowed night robe flapping about his thin legs, he seized one of the books lying on the table.

'I had no idea your majesty would be back so soon!' he cried, flipping pages rapidly. 'There is something I must show you! Something of great importance.'

'I would like to see everything in its turn, Josef,' Lief said hastily. 'But just now I have some research of my own that—'

He heard a slight sound behind him and turned to meet the shrewd, hazel eyes of a dark man with a humorous twist to his mouth.

This, Lief knew, must be Ranesh, Josef's apprentice. How silently he had approached! Unlike Josef, he had taken the time to dress before leaving his room at the back of the library. Perhaps that said something about the difference in their characters.

Ranesh was a man who would not rush to anyone's bidding. He was a man who would weigh his decisions carefully. A man whose real character it would be difficult to know.

A man like Doom, thought Lief, glancing at his friend.

Doom was watching the newcomer. Lief knew that he was trying to decide if Ranesh was to be trusted

'We should have tidied this table before going to our beds, I know,' Josef was chattering, still searching his book. 'But I wished to clean the shelves before arranging the *Annals*. I fear the library has been sadly neglected. Then I became very tired, and—'

'Of course!' Lief said, in a frenzy to have time alone with the precious books. 'I am sorry that our arrival woke you, Josef. And you, too, Ranesh. Please return to your rest. We are quite able to—'

'Ah, here it is!' Josef cried. He placed the open book on the table and pulled out a chair. 'Read, your majesty!' he begged. 'And here—' He pushed forward paper and a pencil. 'You can take notes with these, if you wish, as young Jasmine did this afternoon.'

'*Jasmine*?' Lief exclaimed. 'She was *reading*?'

'Oh, yes!' Josef nodded. 'She was taking notes from the *Annals*.'

'From volume 1,' Ranesh put in. 'I happened to notice before she closed it.'

Ah, yes, you *would* notice, Ranesh, thought Lief. There is not much those sharp eyes miss, I fancy. He glanced at Doom's expressionless face, knowing that Doom was wondering, as he was, whether Jasmine had somehow also heard of the Pirran Pipe.

'Now, your majesty,' urged Josef, waving at the open book. 'Will you read—?'

'Certainly I will, Josef, but only if you and Ranesh leave us,' said Lief, trying with all his might to keep his voice casual and unhurried. 'I will not be able to concentrate if I know I am keeping you awake.'

Josef hesitated, his eyes flicking from the open book to Lief's face and back again.

'We will speak again soon,' Lief added, forcing a smile.

At last Josef nodded. Plucking at Ranesh's sleeve to make sure his assistant followed his lead, he bowed and shuffled away.

Soon Lief and Doom heard the sound of their mumured goodnights, and doors closing at the back of the library.

'At last!' Lief breathed. 'Now—to find this tale.'

He swung round to the table. The book lay open at the place the old librarian had been so anxious for him to see.

Lief glanced impatiently at the yellowed pages, the small, exquisitely neat printing. A name caught his eye. He gasped and stared.

'Doom!' he whispered. 'Look!'

THE TALE OF THE PIRRAN PIPE

Long, long ago, beyond the Mountains, there was a green land called Pirra, where the breezes breathed magic. Jealous Shadows lurked on Pirra's borders, but the land was protected by a mysterious Pipe, which played notes of such beauty that no evil could take root within sound of its voice.

The Pipe was played morning, noon and evening by the people's chief, the Piper, who was the finest player in the land.

One dark winter's night, the Piper of those days passed away in her sleep. The next day, three great musicians offered themselves as her replacement. They were called Plume the Brave, Auron the Fair and Keras the Unknown.

The three played in turn before the people, as was the custom. Plume's playing was so stirring that the crowd cheered. Auron's music was so beautiful that her audience wept. Keras created sounds so haunting that all who heard them were rapt in wonder.

When the people voted to choose their favourite, each player received an equal number of votes. The three played again, and again. But each time the result was the same.

Night fell, but the testing went on. The people, who had by now separated into three groups according to their favourite, grew tired and angry. But each person wanted his or her own choice to become Piper, and would not vote for another.

At last, long after midnight, when the vote was called equal for the thirteenth time, the three groups turned furiously upon one another, using their magic to insult and injure.

A man in a hooded cloak stepped forward. He was tall, but bent with weakness, as though the long day and night of music had been almost beyond his endurance. Each section of the crowd thought that he was one of its own, for he had spent time with all three, urging its members to hold firm.

'I have a solution, my friends!' he cried. 'Let the contestants share the honour of being Piper. The Pipe is made from three parts which fit together. Let Plume, Auron and Keras each take one part of the whole.'

And so tired, so angry had the people become that they agreed. They gave Plume the mouthpiece of the Pipe, Auron the middle stem, and Keras the endpiece. Then, because they still had bad feelings for one another, the three groups went their separate ways, each group following its own favourite.

The hooded man rubbed his hands, well satisfied, and slipped away like a shadow before the rising of the sun.

The dawn broke with no sound of music and the long day passed in silence, for the three rival groups were far apart, and no one piece of the Pirran Pipe could play alone.

Shadows crept into Pirra. Trees withered in their shade and flowers wilted. Little by little the Shadows swallowed up the green fields, the pleasant villages, while every moment the dread power cloaked within them grew stronger.

Too late, the three groups realised their danger. Shadows now rolled dark between them. They could not reach one another to make the magic Pipe whole. And at last, seeing that their land was lost, they were forced to to use the last of their magic to escape, and save themselves.

So it was that the green land of Pirra became the Shadowlands. Its people, still blaming one another for their ancient loss, dwell to this day on three separate islands in a strange and secret sea.

And the Pirran Pipe, forever divided, is heard no more.

9 - Grains of Truth

Doom drew back from the table. 'So—the Shadow Lord played the same trick on Pirra as he did on Deltora. He divided the people, made the land's protection useless, then invaded.'

'The Pirrans allowed him to do it,' Lief muttered, rubbing his hand over his eyes. 'As we in Deltora did in our turn. He used their anger, their stubbornness, their ambition, their weakness . . .'

'Your majesty!'

A white figure was hobbling slowly towards them from the back of the library. Josef.

'Forgive me, your majesty,' the old man mumbled, as he drew closer. 'But I forgot—'

Lief scrambled to his feet and held out his hand. 'Forgive *me*, Josef,' he said. 'You were trying to tell me of the Pirran Pipe, and I would not listen.'

Josef's face lit with an eager smile as he took the offered hand. 'You have read the Tale, then?' he whispered. 'You believe it contains a grain of truth?'

At Lief's nod, he hurried on. 'I am sure that each of the Pirran tribes would have treasured its own part of the Pipe, and kept it safe. So if the Pirrans still exist, the three parts of the Pirran Pipe exist also.'

'I am as sure of it as you are,' said Lief. 'And I know the Pipe can help us, for I have heard its voice.'

Josef stared at him, awe-struck. 'You must understand, your majesty,' he ventured at last, 'that the Enemy has the Shadowlands too firmly in his grasp now for even the Pirran Pipe to drive him out of it. All the Pipe could do, I believe, is weaken him.'

'I understand,' Lief said firmly. 'Do not fear, Josef. All we hope for is time—time to get our prisoners out! But first we must find the Pirran Islands.'

'Yes!' Josef cried. 'That is what I had forgotten to tell you!' Swiftly he seized volume 5 of the *Annals* and expertly riffled through the back pages. In a very short time he had found what he was seeking: a series of maps.

He pointed to a small sketch above another, much larger, map of the western sea.

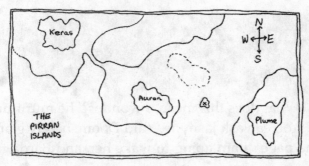

'There is no signature, but I strongly suspect this sketch was made by Doran, our greatest explorer,' Josef said. 'He certainly drew the larger map below. I recognise his hand. '

'Thank you, Josef.' Lief's heart was too full to say more. The map was so simple as to be almost useless. But to him it proved one thing at least. The Pirran Islands were not just a legend. They existed. And that meant they could be found.

Josef beamed. 'It is my pleasure to be of service,' he said. He bowed, turned, and tottered back to his room.

Lief reached for the paper and pencil. 'I will trace this map,' he said. 'Perhaps we can find others with which to compare it.'

He looked down at the sheaf of paper in front of him. Now that it was in better light, he could see that the top page bore indented marks caused by Jasmine writing heavily on a sheet of paper above it.

He rubbed the side of the pencil tip lightly over the white surface. As he had hoped, the grooves in its surface began to show as white lines.

'What does this mean, I wonder?' he murmured.

'You can ask Jasmine,' said Doom, barely glancing at the page. 'I am going to wake her, and Barda too. If they are to accompany me on this voyage . . .'

Lief looked up quickly. 'Accompany *us*, you mean,' he said. 'I am going with you. Do you really think the Pirrans will give up their greatest treasure to anyone other than the king of Deltora?'

Doom frowned. 'You are right,' he said at last. 'The king must be the one to ask the favour. But you must agree to this, Lief—Jasmine, Barda and I will be the ones to take the risks, if risks there be.'

Lief nodded reluctantly. Doom lightly touched his shoulder, and left him.

Alone, Lief stared again at Jasmine's strange words. They made him uneasy. 'O-M hills' must mean the dangerous Os-Mine Hills, to the north of Del. But what the rest meant he could not imagine.

Ranesh had said that Jasmine was reading Volume 1 of the *Annals*—the very book open before him now. Lief began turning pages, finding more Tenna Birdsong Tales. *The Tale of the Three Knights*. *The Seven Goblins*. *The Dragon's Egg* . . .

Then he found something else. Caught between two pages was a small black feather.

Kree! Lief imagined the great black bird sitting on the book as Jasmine read. He imagined Kree fluttering back as Jasmine closed the book hurriedly, on Josef's approach. And a feather falling, to be trapped between the pages.

He read the story on the open double page with a growing sense of dread.

THE GIRL WITH THE GOLDEN HAIR

Once there was a maiden called Alyss, whose only beauty was her long, golden hair which shone like the sun. Though her eyes were small, her nose was very long and her ears were as big as bat's wings, her golden tresses were so beautiful that she had many admirers. She encouraged all except one, a youth called Rosnan, who was as plain as she.

One day, Alyss was combing her hair, to the delight of all who watched her, when a great, golden dragon swooped from the sky and carried her off.

All her handsome admirers wept, and gave her up for lost, but Rosnan took his sword and followed the dragon to its cave in a valley of the Os-Mine Hills. Seeing him, the dragon snarled and breathed fire, but Rosnan stood firm.

'Free Alyss, great dragon!' he cried. 'Take me instead!'

The dragon laughed—a truly terrible sound that made even the vine weaver birds in the trees above fall silent. 'You will not do!' it said. 'Have you golden hair to line my nest? I do not think so.'

With that, it flicked its tail and sent Rosnan sprawling, the sword falling, useless, to the ground. 'Run Alyss!' shouted Rosnan, as he prepared for death. 'Save yourself!'

But Alyss picked up the fallen sword and, with a single sweep, cut off her hair. 'Take it!' she cried to the dragon, holding out the golden silk, so long and thick that it filled her arms. 'But let him live!'

The dragon turned away from Rosnan, and its eyes shone with pleasure as it took the hair. 'Thank you,' it said.

'I will.'

Then Alyss saw herself in the mirror of the dragon's eyes, and was so horrified at her ugliness that she screamed and ran. She ran deep into the dragon's cave and down, down under the earth, into the caverns where the goblins dwell. Calling after her, Rosnan followed, but Alyss did not stop, for gold light gleamed in the cavern walls, tormenting her and reminding her of what she had lost.

They fled—Alyss in front, Rosnan behind—through the sunless world below the world, where the seas of forgetfulness crawl. They fled so far that they forgot why they were fleeing, but they went without harm, for they were so ugly that the goblins mistook them for a pair of their own.

The gleaming gold changed to red that glowed like the setting sun. Then came glimmering rainbows, and the green of the forest after rain. And still the chase went on.

But when the colour faded to the grey of dusk, and the darkness of deepest night was ahead, Alyss feared to go further, and stopped. Then Rosnan caught up with her and took her in his arms, saying that to him she was the most beautiful girl in the world. Which was nothing but the truth, for he loved her with all his heart.

And Alyss looked at him and saw a soul that was honest, brave and true. And her heart melted within her.

The goblins saw their love, and wondered at its power. A few travelled to the world above, seeking the same happiness for themselves, though never finding it. But the lovers were never seen under the sun again, and only the birds know that, deep in the world below the world, they lived happily ever after.

Lief sat for a moment, deep in thought. Then he heard a sound from the door. Doom and Barda were striding towards him, grim-faced. He knew what they had come to tell him before they spoke.

'Jasmine has gone, hasn't she?' he asked dully.

They looked surprised, but did not ask how he knew.

'Her bed has not been slept in.' Barda rubbed his forehead angrily. 'She slipped away yesterday, no doubt, while I was asleep. I should have expected this! By now she will be in the Forests. And alone!'

Lief shook his head. 'Not alone,' he replied. 'If I am right, Glock is with her. And they have not gone to the Forests, but to the Os-Mine Hills. I believe—I am sure—that Jasmine thinks she has found a secret way to the Shadowlands. Underground.'

10 - Pursuit

Marilen shivered and wrapped her cloak more closely around her. It was not yet dawn, but Lief knew that she was shuddering not with cold, but with anxiety she was trying desperately to disguise.

'Do not fear, Marilen,' he said gently. 'You need do nothing but wait. Doom is staying here, to prepare for a journey. He will watch over you. And Barda and I will soon return.'

He hoped that she would not ask him where he was going. Even in Tora, she might have heard the evil stories of the Os-Mine Hills. He smothered a sigh of relief as she nodded silently.

'I had not planned to leave you so soon,' Lief went on carefully. 'But I do not think that Jasmine will return for anyone but me, for I am the one who offended her.'

'I do understand, Lief,' Marilen said in a low voice. 'And you must not think I am a coward, who will always panic as soon as you leave her sight.'

Torn between fury at Jasmine's stubbornness, and a terrible fear for her safety, Lief was impatient to be gone. But there was one thing left to ask.

'Very few people know that we returned with Doom last night, Marilen,' he said. 'Most think we are still in Tora. It is safest if they continue in this belief for now. Will you remain out of sight while I am gone? Mother will see to your meals.'

Marilen raised her eyes to meet his anxious gaze. 'Do not worry about me, Lief,' she said quietly. 'I will occupy myself in the library.'

Lief smiled, hiding his doubts. He had not remembered the library. But he could not bring himself to forbid it to Marilen.

As he left her, he told himself that all would be well. The guards would not allow Marilen to stray into the forbidden hallway. And Josef could surely be trusted to keep her presence secret.

What of Ranesh? Doubts stirred again, but Lief forced them out of his mind, and hurried down the stairs.

He was approaching the kitchen, where he had arranged to meet Barda, when he heard a muffled scream. He quickened his pace and as he threw open the door a startling sight met his eyes.

Barda had Jinks by the collar, and was shaking him. Jinks, wearing a red nightshirt, his mouth smeared with jam, was howling, trying to kick the big man's legs.

'You knew they had gone, you miserable worm!' Barda was thundering. 'Yet you said *nothing*!'

'Am I Glock's keeper?' screeched Jinks. 'He is old enough and ugly enough to look after himself. And as for that green-eyed minx he went with—'

His voice broke off in a high-pitched squeal as Barda jerked him upward, nearly strangling him.

'Barda, put him down!' Lief begged. 'He will wake the whole palace!'

Barda swung around, hauling Jinks with him. Jinks' eyes widened. 'I did not know you were home, your majesty!' he spluttered. 'Call off your bear, I beg you. He has gone wild!'

'I can go wilder yet, Jinks,' growled Barda. 'Do not tempt me. Would you care to explain to "your majesty" why you were stealing food while the rest of us tighten our belts and eat only our fair share?'

'I am in delicate health,' Jinks whimpered. 'I need frequent small, tasty morsels to keep body and soul together.'

'Indeed?' said Lief coldly.

'I found him guzzling jam,' said Barda, looking at Jinks with contempt. 'To get himself out of trouble, he accused Glock and Jasmine of being traitors.'

'It was very wrong of them to set out for the Shadowlands when your majesty has forbidden it,' whined Jinks to Lief. 'Why, torn as I was between loyalty to them and loyalty to your majesty, it is no wonder that I became dizzy, and needed a taste of sweetness.'

Barda snorted. Lief moved closer to Jinks. 'Glock and Jasmine are free to go where they wish,' he said.

'We are simply concerned for their safety. Do you know the way they have taken?'

'They did not take the trouble to inform me,' Jinks snapped, forgetting that he was supposed to be ill.

His face creased into a furious scowl. 'That animal Glock cares nothing for anyone else's comfort! My fighting spider lost to his in our last contest, and is mad for revenge. She kept me awake all night, beating at her cage. That is why I needed—'

'Jinks!' Lief began in exasperation. But Barda's voice, tight with excitement, drowned him out.

'Glock took his spider with him, then?' he snapped.

'Yes,' said Jinks sullenly. 'And what if he is away for weeks? Or never returns at all? What am I—?'

He squeaked as Barda began to haul him towards the door. 'Where are we going?' he cried in panic. 'Not the dungeons, surely? It was just a few spoonfuls of jam! Your majesty! Stop him! Have mercy!'

'Be silent!' growled Barda. 'I am not taking you to the dungeons, you fool. You are going to dress and put your spider on its chain. Then you are coming with us.'

✦

The journey to the Os-Mine Hills was the strangest Lief had ever made.

Barda held the whining Jinks on the saddle in front of him. Jinks held the end of a long, fine chain. And at the other end of the chain, scurrying in front of the horses, was a huge, spotted brown spider called Fury.

'Fighting spiders cannot stand defeat,' Barda

explained to Lief as they rode. 'A losing spider will not rest until it has tracked the victor and forced it to fight again. Fury will follow Glock's spider's scent to the end of the earth, given the chance. She is our best hope of finding Glock—and Jasmine—quickly.'

It was soon clear that Lief had been right in believing that Jasmine was aiming for the Os-Mine Hills. Without hesitation, Fury was leading them towards those ragged peaks regarded with dread by all in Del.

She moved so fast that the horses, picking their way over the rough ground, could hardly keep up with her. When she was forced to stop, she fought furiously to continue.

At night she beat ceaselessly against the sides of the cage in which Jinks kept her while he slept. Not that Jinks, or either of his companions, *could* sleep. It was truly astonishing that a single spider, however large, could make such a din.

The second day brought them to the first low, rocky ridges of the Os-Mine Hills. The way was even more difficult for the horses now, and Fury strained on her chain as the pace of her followers slowed.

'We might do better on foot,' said Barda, as his horse stumbled for the third time in an hour.

'No!' Jinks squealed. He squirmed in the saddle, his face a picture of fear. 'This is Granous country! Have you not heard the stories?'

'Of course,' Barda said grimly. 'But so has everyone else. That is why there are no trails through this wilderness. On foot we can at least follow Fury more safely.'

Jinks opened his mouth to argue, but his words were never spoken. For abruptly a grey shape streaked from the bushes in front of them, sharp, yellow teeth snapped, and the horses reared, shrieking with pain and fright, tumbling their startled riders to the ground.

✦

As Lief slowly came to his senses, he became aware that he was sitting on the ground, tied to a tree at the edge of a clearing. Something was panting close to his face. Its hot breath was foul.

Lief opened his eyes and saw grinning jaws, grey, matted fur, a wet, snuffling black nose. With sinking heart he realised that this must be a Granous. And there were more of them—several more, by the sound of the other mutterings and gigglings in the background.

The creature which had filled his vision moved back and squatted on the ground. Now Lief could see its companions—four of them. All had the same evil grins on their faces. Every now and then, one of them would snap its yellow teeth unpleasantly.

Lief struggled to free himself, but at once realised that it was impossible. His ankles were tied to pegs that had been driven into the ground. His wrists were lashed to heavy logs of wood that lay on either side of him. His sword was still at his belt, but he could not reach it.

Turning his head, he saw that Barda and Jinks were tied exactly as he was. Barda was still shouting furiously.

Jinks' jaw was gaping, his eyes mad with fear, the remains of Fury's chain dangling from his wrist.

Fury's chain must have broken when Jinks fell, thought Lief. She will catch up to Jasmine and Glock without us. Perhaps she already has. Again he vainly struggled against his bonds. They were only vines, but were as strong as the heaviest rope.

'Free us, Granous, or it will be the worse for you!' roared Barda.

Their captors laughed uproariously. 'It will be the worse for you!' mimicked one. 'Oh, I am so afraid!'

'This is Lief, king of Deltora!' Barda growled, jerking his head at Lief. 'You dare not harm him!'

'We care nothing for kings,' sneered the first Granous, who seemed to be the leader. 'The dragons have gone. These are *our* hills now.'

It grinned at Lief, and bowed mockingly. 'But if you are a king, *you* can be the one to play the Twenty Questions game with us. We have never matched wits with a king before.'

Its shaggy companions grinned, snuffled and snapped their jaws. A chill ran down Lief's spine.

The first Granous moved closer, rubbing its hands together. Tufts of grey fur covered the backs of the hands. The fingers were thin as wires, tipped by nails that were long, yellow and rimmed with grime

Lief stared in fascinated horror. His own fingers tingled at the thought of those hands grasping his, the sharp teeth moving closer . . .

'Rules are simple, king,' said the Granous, grinning horribly. 'We ask question, you answer. If answer is wrong, you pay the price. One finger from you, and one from each of your friends. Yes?'

Jinks began to wail piteously.

Fighting for calm, Lief concentrated on the birds chattering in the trees that surrounded the clearing. No doubt they were Os-Mine vine weaver birds, of which he had learned as a child. Their famous net-like nests strung many of the treetops.

He breathed deeply, feeling Barda's eyes upon him. He knew that Barda was hoping against hope that the gems of the Belt of Deltora would help them now. The topaz that sharpened the mind. The amethyst that calmed. The diamond that gave strength . . .

He swallowed. 'What if I will not play?' he asked.

The Granous shrugged. 'If you do not answer in the time it takes to count twenty, you lose. And you each give a finger. Then we ask another question. And so on. You see?'

Lief saw only too well.

'And if I answer correctly?' he asked.

'Then no finger is taken,' said the Granous, 'And we ask another question. At the end of twenty questions, you are all free to leave us.' Its face split into another hideous grin. 'If you can,' it added. 'For when the fingers are finished, we begin on the toes.'

Jinks' wails grew louder.

11 - A Friend in Need

The head Granous placed a small wooden board on Lief's lap. The board was very old, and beautifully crafted. Many squares of wood, each one bearing a painted letter, had been arranged upon it in rows.

'Where did you get this?' Lief exclaimed.

'We have had many visitors before you, king!' the Granous giggled. 'Now! Your first question is—what are the only useful things about you? The answer is hidden on the board. It may run up, down, sideways, or all three. Go!'

At once, the other Granous began to clap and chant. 'Twenty. Nineteen. Eighteen . . .'

Lief stared at the board. The letters seemed to swim before his eyes. He blinked, trying to clear his head, searching desperately for a starting point.

Words seemed to jump out at him. GET. TIN. BENT. BASE. PAN. But they led nowhere.

Up, down, sideways, or all three . . .

'. . . Fourteen. Thirteen. Twelve. . .' The counting was growing louder.

Lief glanced desperately at Barda. Barda, squinting at the board, trying to make the letters out at a distance, shook his head. Beyond him, Jinks, his face fixed in concentration and shiny with sweat, was staring straight ahead. But then Lief saw that one of the acrobat's hands, narrowed to a claw, was moving—twisting rapidly.

Jinks was trying one of his old tricks. And this time it was not for the entertainment of others, or for a bet, but to save his life. He was trying to slip out of his bonds while the Granous were not watching him. Lief looked quickly back at the board, his heart thumping.

The Granous leader pretended to smother a yawn, tapping its gaping mouth with its hand. The wicked teeth were razor sharp. Sharp enough to shear through flesh and snap through bone.

The only good things about you . . .

An idea flashed into Lief's mind. Feverishly he searched the board.

'Six. Five. Four . . .'

And suddenly, there was the answer, coiled within the mass of letters, crooked as a snake.

'Ten fingers and ten toes!' Lief shouted.

The chanting stopped, dissolving into a chorus of disappointed groans.

Lief risked another glance at Jinks. The little man had managed to free his hand, and was cautiously feeling for the dagger at his belt.

'No doubt you think you are very clever, king,' said the first Granous sulkily. 'We will see. Here is your second question. Listen carefully.'

It folded its hands over its belly, and recited:

A king dined with his sister,
His friend and his friend's wife.
All of them were greedy beasts
Who loved food more than life.
At last three pies alone remained.
There wasn't any knife.
How did they all have equal shares,
And save themselves from strife?

The chorus of counting began again. Lief tried to forget about Jinks and concentrate on the rhyme.

Three pies. No knife. Equal shares for four people. It sounded impossible! But he knew that such apparently impossible puzzles always contained a simple trick.

The chanting of the Granous pounded on.

'...TWELVE. ELEVEN. TEN ...'

'Lief!' Barda whispered urgently. 'Perhaps one of the four was killed by the others. The verse says they loved food more than life.'

Lief shook his head. 'It says they *all* had equal shares,' he whispered back. 'All of them. The king, his sister, his friend and ...

A thought stirred in the back of his mind.

'...FIVE! FOUR! ...'

Barda cursed under his breath.

'THREE! TWO! ...'

'The king's sister was married to his friend!' Lief cried. '*That* is how the pies were equally divided. There were only three people at dinner all the time!'

This time the counting broke off in howls of frustration. The head Granous scowled as the others began shouting at him, criticising his choice of questions.

Lief slumped back, pretending relief, and slid his half closed eyes in the direction of Jinks' tree.

The acrobat had gone! The vines with which he had been bound were lying loose on the ground. He must be even now creeping through the bushes behind Lief and Barda, dagger at the ready to cut their bonds.

Hurry, Jinks! thought Lief. The Granous were still arguing, paying no attention to the prisoners. Jinks would never have a better chance than this.

Barda drew a sharp, hissing breath. His eyes were fixed on a rocky hill that could just be seen over the trees on the other side of the clearing. Lief followed his gaze.

A small figure was scrambling up the hill. Jinks!

Far from remaining to save his companions, Jinks was running away as fast as he could.

One of the Granous suddenly screeched and pointed. 'Prisoner escaped!' it howled. Instantly the whole group plunged off into the bushes, following the acrobat's scent.

'I hope they catch him, the vile little worm!' muttered Barda, struggling violently against the vines that bound him. 'How could he leave us here?'

A vine weaver bird flew down from the tree above Barda and perched on the log to which his right hand was tied. It put its head on one side, and regarded him with a sharp black eye.

It nodded as if satisfied. Then it hopped onto his wrist and began pecking at the knotted vine.

'Lief!' Barda whispered in astonishment. 'Look!'

The knots were loosening! The bird's long, expert beak was doing what all Barda's strength could not.

In moments, his right hand was free. The bird began working on the knots that bound him to the tree while he sliced through his other bonds with his sword.

He scrambled stiffly to his feet, and staggered over

to cut Lief loose. Then, with the vine weaver swooping ahead of them, they both stumbled out of the clearing and into the undergrowth.

The bird darted on, plainly expecting them to follow. Even when the ground began to climb steeply it did not slow, whistling impatiently whenever they paused for breath.

At last they reached the top of the hill and slumped to the ground, panting. The air was filled with bird calls, and when Lief raised his head he saw why.

Not far below them was a thick mass of treetops, ringed by the peaks of other grey hills. Birds in their thousands were busily weaving their nets or feeding on the yellow berries that covered the trees.

Lief and Barda's guide darted around their heads, calling urgently.

It is foolish to think that the bird is leading us to Jasmine, Lief told himself as they followed it down to ground level. Jasmine is searching for a valley, not a high-ground forest.

But hope still flickered as he followed Barda into the trees, his feet sinking deep into the thick carpet of rotting leaves that covered the forest floor.

Then he saw, just ahead, dozens of birds swooping around a small bush which was thrashing violently from side to side for no apparent reason. The vine weaver sped towards the place.

And there, her chain caught around the bush, was Fury.

She was living up to her name—twisting and lunging, her huge fangs snapping. Her trailing chain had become tangled around the bush, and was holding her fast.

Lief swallowed his disappointment. The vine weaver, it seemed, thought one good turn deserved another. It had freed them. Now it wanted them to remove this unwelcome visitor from its forest.

In moments Barda had untangled the chain. The instant Fury felt it loosening she made a wild dash foward, almost jerking him off his feet. Lief felt hope flare all over again.

'She is still following a scent!' he shouted over the excited shrilling of the birds. 'Glock's spider must have passed this way!'

With a call of thanks to their relieved vine weaver guide, they plunged after Fury into the trees.

As they moved deeper into the forest it grew darker and more silent. The only living creatures to be seen were fat, gold-coloured moths that blundered about in the dimness like stray scraps of sunlight.

For a long time, Fury did not pause. Then, abruptly, she stopped. She rose up on her back legs, her fangs clicking together, her front legs frozen in the air.

'What is she doing?' Lief whispered.

He and Barda moved cautiously forward. Several of the big yellow moths were fluttering close to the ground just beyond where Fury was poised.

'She must be hungry,' said Barda.

Fury lowered her front legs once more and began creeping towards the moths. She had almost reached them when Lief noticed something odd.

There were more moths than before. Yet he had not seen any new ones fly down to join the crowd.

Then he realised what was happening. The moths were fluttering around a hole in the ground. And more moths were rising out of the hole every moment.

'They must lay their eggs down there,' murmured Barda. He shouted in annoyance as Fury suddenly jumped forward and scuttled into the hole, disappearing deep inside.

The moths scattered, bumbling out of the way. Barda tugged vainly at the spider's chain, cursing it and ordering it to come back. But Lief's heart was thumping as he threw himself to the ground, scraped the disguising piles of leaves away from the sides of the hole and peered into its depths.

When he looked up his eyes were shining.

'Barda!' he exclaimed. 'Barda—you are not going to believe this!'

And without another word, he swung his legs into the hole, and followed Fury.

12 - Mysteries

Barda bent over the hole, roaring furiously. But Lief, rapidly disappearing into the gloom, merely shouted to him to follow. Fury plainly had no intention of returning to ground level either. The chain around Barda's wrist was pulling violently.

There was only one thing to do. Barda scrambled into the hole himself, cursing under his breath. What was the boy doing? What had he seen in this foul burrow?

Dirt and rotted leaves showered his face as he lowered himself through the earth, clinging to the tree roots that netted the sides of the hole. His feet scrabbled for footholds. His hands ached. When he looked up, he could see only a faint glimmer of light.

'Take care!' Lief's muffled voice floated upwards.

'You are a fine one to speak of taking care!' Barda shouted back.

A moment later, his feet broke into open space. He

kicked out wildly, searching for a foothold. Something grabbed his ankles, and he yelled.

'I have you!' Lief called. 'Wait!'

With relief, Barda felt his feet guided to a firm surface. Slowly he lowered himself out of the tunnel.

The first thing he saw was Lief's face, wild with excitement and streaked with dirt. Then he moved his eyes downward. And stared.

He was looking down at a vast space filled with thousands of huge grey poles that stretched from floor to ceiling. A gurgling stream lined with pale ferns wound its way through the poles, disappearing into the dimness.

Then he realised what he was seeing, and his jaw dropped.

'Why, they are giant trees!' he breathed. 'This is a forest! A forest beneath a forest! How could this be?'

'I think the vine weaver birds must have caused it,' said Lief, touching the matted web of branches and vines above his head. 'Once they lived in the tops of these trees, weaving their nests and eating berries. Over time, the forest canopy became so thick and tangled that it was almost solid. The berries the birds dropped did not fall to the ground, but were caught in old nests, and the forks of branches.'

'So the seeds took root, watered by the rain and young trees grew on top of the old,' said Barda. 'And after hundreds of years . . .'

'After hundreds of years,' Lief finished for him,

'there was no sign of the old forest left. No sign of the valley in which it grew. Only the trees, the moths and the birds above knew the secret.'

Barda became aware that Fury was tugging once more on her chain. She had moved down the tree as far as she could, and was now rearing and scrabbling in frustration because she could go no further.

'We still do not know if Jasmine and Glock are here, or just Glock's spider,' he said.

Lief grinned. 'What trees and birds know, Jasmine soon knows also,' he said. 'She and Glock have found this place, there is no doubt. Look!'

He pointed. And there, tied around the trunk of the tree and dangling almost to the ground, was a rope.

✦

It did not take long for Lief and Barda to reach the ground using the rope, but even this small delay drove Fury to distraction. The moment she was free to do so, she set off at a great pace along the stream.

This time, Lief and Barda hardly needed her to show them the way to go. The ground was almost covered by fragile white fungus and patches of brittle fern. The tracks of two people were plainly visible—one set of heavy, large prints, one set of lighter, smaller ones.

The air was heavy with the smell of earth and mould. There was no sound but the gurgling of the stream. The trees rose silent and ghostly around them, their trunks blotched with tongues of yellow fungus from which hung squirming bundles of fat caterpillars.

Clearly the moths from the forest above used the hidden valley as a safe nesting place.

Now and then Lief or Barda called Jasmine's name, but no answering cry reached their ears. Slowly a feeling of dread began to grow in Lief. Were they too late? Words from *The Girl with the Golden Hair* echoed in his mind.

She ran deep into the dragon's cave and down, down under the earth, into the caverns where the goblins live . . .

'Dragons have been extinct in Deltora for hundreds of years,' said Barda, as if reading his mind. 'If there is a dragon's lair in this valley, it is empty. The forest would never have been covered over if this was not so. The dragon would have kept the canopy open, by flying out to hunt every day.'

'And the goblins?' muttered Lief. 'Are they extinct also?'

'If they ever existed,' said Barda. 'My mother used to tell a story of seven goblins who prowled the countryside north of Del. But the tale always began, "Once upon a time", as fairy stories do.'

'I have heard Glock claim that one of his ancestors fought and killed a goblin,' said Lief.

Barda snorted. 'I have heard Glock claim many things,' he said.

They rounded a bend in the stream and saw ahead of them a rocky cliff, rising behind the trees like a wall. The stream ended in a small, deep pool at its foot.

'We have reached the forest's edge,' whispered

Barda. 'This must be the base of one of the hills we saw when we looked down from the other side.'

Lief nodded, his skin prickling as he saw that the footprint trail led away from the stream, and into a vast, dark cave in the cliff.

Fury dashed ahead of them as they crept towards the cave's entrance. It was heavily fringed with ferns, and somehow this made it look even more like a gaping, toothless mouth. Inside, it was black as night and silent as the grave.

'Lief,' Barda breathed. 'The ruby . . .'

Reluctantly Lief pulled his cloak aside to reveal the jewelled belt. The rich red of the ruby seemed only a little dimmer.

'If there is danger, it is slight,' Barda said, visibly relaxing.

Lief wet his lips. 'I think we should still take care,' he said slowly. 'The belt may not be as powerful here as it is on the surface. And look at Fury.'

Barda glanced downward. The huge spider was standing motionless and wary at his feet.

They lit a torch. Then, shoulder to shoulder, swords drawn, they moved into the cave.

The torch lit the ground immediately ahead, but thick darkness surrounded its warm, flickering glow. It was as though they were floating through a black sea in a small bubble of light.

Lief felt as though he was moving in a dream. The air was heavy and warm. And slowly, slowly, a strange, musky smell was growing in strength.

'There is something alive in here,' he breathed.

As he spoke, the torchlight flickered on something ahead. Something huge.

Scales gleamed golden amid dancing shadows. Teeth and claws glimmered white. A tail lay coiled, thick with spines as sharp as needles. Folded leathery wings netted with spider webs trailed in the dust.

Dragon!

A deep, ancient dread welled up in Lief, turning his legs to jelly. He heard Barda draw a quick breath.

The dragon did not stir. All that moved was the torchlight flickering over its huge form.

'Its eyes are shut. It is asleep—or dead,' Barda hissed.

'Not dead, I think,' said Lief, struggling to calm himself. 'But not asleep either, or it would have sensed us and woken. This is some sort of enchantment.'

Fury began to creep to the left. As Lief and Barda went after her, the torchlight began to flicker on the cave's rocky wall. Soon they saw that there was a narrow space between the wall and the dragon's head.

This then, was to be their path. Already Fury was crawling doggedly through the gap. Taking a deep breath, Barda moved after her, looking straight ahead.

Lief began to follow. He knew that he, too, should keep his eyes to the front, but he could not. He turned and gazed, fascinated, at the terrible head, so near that he had only to stretch out his hand to touch it. And as he stared, the dragon's great, golden eye opened.

Lief froze. His mind went blank. There was no fear, no hope, no thought. There was only the dragon's eye, and his own face mirrored there—pale, weak and small, floating in a cold, flat sea that was gold as the topaz in the Belt of Deltora, deep with ancient memory.

For a long moment the eye held him. Then, slowly, it closed once more.

Released, almost sick with shock, Lief lurched on to where Barda was waiting for him.

'Why did you stop?' Barda whispered. 'Are you mad, Lief, that you would risk—?'

Lief brushed past blindly. Blackness yawned ahead, but that was better than what lay behind him. Cool air fanned his face, chilling the sweat on his brow. All he could think of was to get away—hide himself.

He heard Barda hurrying after him, felt Barda trying to hold him back. There was another gust of cold air. The torch flared and went out.

Lief stumbled, righted himself, and stepped forward into—thin air. There was a split second of disbelief. And then he was falling, dragging Barda with him, plunging down, down into darkness.

13 - Gold and Scarlet

Deep, chill water. Holding him down. Up! Up! Breathe! His lungs almost bursting, Lief fought his way to the surface. He floundered there, taking great gulps of air, looking blindly around him through a blur of water

'Barda!' he shouted desperately.

Barda ... Barda ... Barda ... Echoes answered him—a thousand echoes, calling and whispering from every direction.

There was a sudden splashing nearby. Dizzy with relief, Lief heard Barda gasping and coughing.

'Barda! I am here!' he called, struggling towards the sound.

Here ... here ... here ...

As his eyes began to clear, Lief saw the shape of Barda's head, dark against water that moved like pale, liquid gold. He saw the soft glow of gold all around him, gold shining from the walls of a vast cavern that seemed to have no beginning and no end.

Gold as the dragon's eye, as the dragon's scales. Gold as the great topaz.

This was the cavern through which Alyss fled in ages past. This was the place Jasmine had sought. The beginning of the underground way to the Shadowlands.

But the old tale had not mentioned one important detail. The cavern was flooded. And . . . Lief's stomach turned over.

And Jasmine could not swim.

Through a haze of misery he saw Barda's arm reach out and catch hold of something that was bobbing in the water beside him. For a terrifying moment Lief thought that it was a body. Then he realised that it was only a log of wood.

He looked up. The shimmering roof of the cavern curved high above him like a golden sky. The hole through which he and Barda had fallen was just a small, blurred patch of darkness. He could barely see it. There was no way he and Barda could reach it.

Barda paddled over to him, half leaning on the log. 'This will keep us afloat for a while at least,' he panted. 'Until we find another way out. Or . . .'

Or what? Lief thought, as his companion's voice faltered. Until finally the wood grows waterlogged, and sinks? Until we grow too exhausted to hold onto it any longer?

'The water may be more shallow further on,' he said huskily. 'Let us try.'

As he spoke, he saw movement out of the corner of his eye. Something small and dark was wriggling towards them through the rippling water. Lief could hardly believe his eyes when he recognised the tangle of flailing legs and angry red stare for what they were.

'Fury!' he exclaimed, as the spider reached the log.

Fury climbed laboriously from the water, still trailing a short length of chain. She reached the top of the log and crouched there glowering, the picture of rage.

Barda shook his head in disbelief. 'I thought that at least I was rid of you, spider,' he growled.

All the same, Fury's appearance had cheered both of them. Supporting themselves on the log, they began to paddle slowly forward.

At first they spoke to one another, marvelling at the mysterious beauty of the place, even joking about Fury's continued sulking. But as the hours passed the talk grew less, and at last they were silent.

It was the silence of exhaustion, cold, and the gradual disappearance of hope. Lief's legs were numb. He no longer had the strength to paddle. He put his head down on the log, feeling its strange, spongy softness under his cheek.

'Lief, hold on! You must not die . . .'

Barda's voice seemed very far away. Lief could not answer. His mind was drifting, floating. As he was drifting on this shining water. As his reflection had floated on the surface of the dragon's eye . . .

✦

Lief swam slowly up from the depths of a fainting sleep with no idea of how much time had passed. He opened his eyes. And blinked.

The golden light had changed to scarlet. The very air seemed stained with red. He could hear the splashing of water, and had the sense of rapid movement.

Slowly it came to him that he was in the bottom of a boat. Barda was lying beside him. And sitting in the centre of the boat, dipping paddles into the water in fast and perfect time, were two strange-looking creatures.

Their bodies were small, but human. Probably, when they stood up, they would be about as tall as gnomes, though they were far less stockily built. But they seemed totally hairless, and their heads and faces were dog-like, with long muzzles and large pointed ears.

At first Lief thought they were dressed in red, and that their skin was red, too. Then he realised that this was an illusion caused by the scarlet glow. In fact, the creatures' skin was deathly pale, with the softness common to crawling things that live beneath the earth.

Lief shuddered. These must be goblins, the ugly, spiteful creatures of old tales, though they did not look as he had imagined.

Unwilling to reveal that he had woken, he watched through half-closed eyelids as the goblins paddled silently, their pale eyes staring straight ahead.

It occurred to him that they were hurrying. There was urgency in their movements, in their set faces. It must have taken some time for them to load Lief and

Barda into their boat. Now, it seemed, they were late, or in some kind of danger.

It was always said that goblins were creatures of evil will. Yet this pair had saved him and Barda from drowning, even though they could ill afford the delay.

Perhaps the goblins' evil reputation was false. Perhaps the few Deltorans who had seen goblins in past ages had feared them simply because of their strange appearance.

But as the thought came to him, Lief felt for his sword. It was missing. He turned his head and saw that Barda's sword, too, was gone. Squinting through the soft red light, he caught the glimmer of metal at the goblins' feet.

He and Barda had been disarmed. Was this just caution on the goblins' part? Or did it mean something more sinister?

A low, rasping sound, like rock grating on rock, echoed through the cavern. The goblins both paused, their ears quivering, their faces alert.

One murmured to the other. Then they both began paddling even faster. The rippling of the water against the boat grew louder as the craft picked up speed.

The rasping sound came again, there was a distant thundering crash and suddenly, shockingly, the nose of the boat rose sharply then dipped again. Lief gasped as cold water slopped over the sides and poured over him. Barda stirred and groaned.

The goblins glanced at them but did not stop

paddling for a second. The boat rose and fell sickeningly once more. And now Lief could see great waves of red water heaving around them, clearly visible over the sides of the boat and becoming larger every moment.

It was as though they were caught in a storm, yet there was no wind. There was only that menacing rasping noise and the dull thundering that was growing louder, and which Lief now recognised as the sound of waves crashing on land.

Land!

He tried to sit up, but fell back again immediately as the boat rose over yet another wave, and slid down the other side. Wallowing in cold, foaming water he struggled to get up again.

'Be still!' cried one of the goblins angrily.

He and his companion were almost knee-deep in swirling water, but still they were paddling with the same fierce concentration as before. Huge red waves were towering over the boat on all sides now, but the goblins looked only ahead, their long noses twitching, their pale eyes staring short-sightedly.

And then, quite suddenly, came a sound and a feeling that made Lief shout with relief. The bottom of the boat was scraping on land.

The goblins threw down their paddles, leaped into the water and began dragging the boat out of the waves, calling for help.

Bruised, shaken and shivering, Lief and Barda crawled to their knees. The goblins were pulling the boat onto muddy land that rose out of the swirling water. Other boats were nearby, tied to what at first seemed strangely-shaped trees, but which Lief soon realised were huge, branching scarlet fungus.

Dazed, Lief looked around him, trying to take in what he was seeing. Hills of red and brown fungus trees, a few nearest the water broken or uprooted by the force of the waves. Orderly fields where rows of some sort of crop showed above streaming water. And beyond the mud of the shore, a village. Waves had crashed over the low wall that surrounded it, and the streets were flooded.

Several goblins were running from the village, crying out in relief and welcome. Lief and Barda's rescuers, whose names seemed to be Clef and Azan, had plainly been anxiously awaited.

But at the sight of Lief and Barda, there was even greater rejoicing, and eager hands helped them out of the boat.

'Get them to safety, quickly,' said Azan, bending to retrieve the swords from behind the boat's seat.

Jostled in the centre of the group, Lief and Barda were hurried towards the village. As they reached the wall the rasping sound came again, this time rising to a high, harsh note that was painful to the ears.

To Lief's surprise, the goblins slowed, and their tense faces relaxed a little. After a moment, he realised that waves were no longer crashing against the walls. The crisis, it seemed, was over. At least for the moment.

They entered the village and began splashing

through empty, flooded streets lined with dwellings.

The houses were all dark red or brown. Many had been damaged by the storm. In other cases, doors had simply burst open, allowing water to stream into the rooms beyond. Brightly painted bowls and pots, small pieces of furniture, even bedding and clothes, drifted in the flood.

Clef peered angrily from side to side as they hurried though street after street. 'This is worse than ever I have seen it!' he growled at last. 'Why has Worron not proceeded with the Giving?'

'There has not been time,' the goblin beside him said nervously. 'The ceremony of preparation had to be begun again for the new Gift, and it is not yet completed.'

'What does that matter?' called Azan from behind. 'That last call was the final warning. Are ceremonies more important than our lives?'

Barda gave a muffled exclamation. Lief glanced at him quickly.

But Barda had not been listening. He was looking over the goblins' heads, towards an open space at the end of the village where a crowd had gathered.

In the centre of the space, clearly visible as the crowd surged forward to greet the newcomers, was a tall cage. It was backed by a high wall and surrounded by a complicated pattern of red stones.

And standing inside the cage, their hands bound behind their backs, were Glock and Jasmine.

14 - The Giving

With a roar, Barda felled the goblins closest to him and swung around, intent on pushing his way towards Azan and the swords. Lief sprang to help him. But before he had taken two steps, there was a brilliant flash and he was frozen to the spot.

At the same moment, the cavern was plunged into darkness. Trembling and blind, his arms and legs refusing to obey his will, Lief stood helpless while confusion reigned around him. The air was filled with cries and moans.

Slowly, very slowly, a little light returned—the faintest red glow, like the promise of sunrise.

Lief began to make out shapes and movement. Barda was standing rigidly nearby, as motionless as Lief was himself. The goblins who had been knocked to the ground were struggling to their feet, with others helping them.

'Bind the creatures, and make haste!' ordered a new

voice. 'I cannot hold them for long and keep the light also.'

With dismay, Lief felt his arms pulled behind his back and his wrists tied together. His ankles, too, were tied, though not so tightly that he could not walk. He saw that Barda was receiving the same treatment.

'Why were they not bound before, Clef?' the new voice demanded irritably. 'Surely you realised that the Longhairs would fight when they saw the Gift?'

'How could they see them from such a distance?' Clef sneered. 'Do they have a magic eye?'

'If you had listened when the old tales were told, boy, you would know that Longhairs have unnaturally far sight,' snapped the other. 'You have endangered us all by your carelessness.'

'And you, Worron, have endangered us all by your delay!' Clef retorted furiously. 'The Giving should have been accomplished long ago. Azan and I were fighting for our lives on the sea while you dallied here, daring the anger of The Fear and allowing the village to be—'

'Do not try to turn attention from your own fault!' cried the goblin called Worron. 'And if you do not respect me, Clef, you can at least respect my office and call me by my proper title.'

Clef kept sullen silence, but through the dimness Lief saw his lips draw away from his teeth in a snarl.

Worron waited for a moment, then raised his voice again. 'I will now release the Longhairs so that we can have more light,' he said. 'Hold them firmly.'

The cavern slowly brightened and Lief felt his arms and legs tingling as movement returned to them. Someone seized his shoulders from behind, and he was turned around. Barda was pushed into place beside him.

Standing before them was a wrinkled goblin wearing a long scarlet robe and a tall, stiff head covering studded with red stones. This, it seemed, was Worron.

Worron leaned forward to peer at the prisoners then abruptly drew back, shuddering slightly and wrinkling his nose. Plainly he found Lief and Barda extremely ugly to look upon, and did not like their smell either.

'Bring them to the Giving Bay,' he said. 'The ceremony must continue at once. The Fear is growing impatient.'

With a swish of his robes, he turned and began hobbling back towards the open space.

Pushed from behind, their arms gripped tightly, Lief and Barda shuffled after him.

Dwarfed by the hulking figure of Glock standing behind her, Jasmine pressed her face against the bars of the cage. Lief's heart lurched.

Kree was sitting on Jasmine's shoulder, and Filli was peeping from her collar. Jasmine's hair was damp and tangled. She looked just as she had looked when Lief first saw her in the Forests of Silence.

But then she had been free. It was agony to see her imprisoned.

Jasmine's eyes were wild as they reached the cage. Clearly she could hardly believe what she was seeing.

'Lief! Barda! What are you doing here?' she burst out. 'How—?'

'Silence!' bellowed Worron. He opened the cage door and beckoned impatiently for Lief and Barda to be pushed inside.

'What are you doing?' shouted Clef angrily, as the order was obeyed. 'Surely you do not intend to use all the Longhairs in the one Giving?'

'Indeed I do,' said Warren. He looked down, clicked his tongue in annoyance and bent down to replace some of the red stones which had been pushed out of place.

'But that is madness!' growled Azan, pushing his way through the crowd to stand by Clef's side. 'The Fear demands only one Gift each year. If we keep three of these Longhairs for the future, our people will not have to draw lots for three more Givings!'

Many in the crowd nodded and murmured agreement.

Worron shook his head disdainfully. 'We cannot keep Longhairs in safety. They are as vicious as they are ugly. Besides—if the Fear is well pleased, it may not demand another Giving for a long time.'

'It is far more likely that it will demand four Gifts instead of one in the future!' cried Clef.

Rumblings of discontent began as Worron continued to tidy the stones, not bothering to reply.

'What are they talking about?' whispered Lief. 'What is The Fear?'

'It is death,' growled Glock.

Wordlessly Jasmine turned and nodded towards a panel in the wall that loomed behind the cage. Lief's stomach lurched as he saw what was carved there.

It was a picture of a terrible sea-beast with ten writhing tentacles. The beast had a screaming goblin in its grasp. It was tearing him apart.

'The Fear is in a cavern called The Glimmer not far from here,' Jasmine murmured. 'Every year it demands a living sacrifice. If the people delay, it beats the water and creates great waves that flood the island and destroy the village. They do not dare to defy it.'

Lief turned and stared in horror at the murmuring crowd gathered outside the cage. He saw Worron straighten and hold up his hands, then press them to his mouth. Silence fell instantly.

Slowly moving his hands forward, the fingertips touching, Worron began a curious, high, wordless singing. Slowly the other goblins joined in. The sound rose and swelled, strangely powerful and thrilling.

'The oldest ones among them draw lots, to see who will be the Gift,' muttered Glock. 'This year it was to be that old crone there.'

He pointed at a bowed and wrinkled goblin who was clutching Clef's arm, urging him to join the singing. Clef frowned and moved away from her, towards the cage. Shaking her head at him, she followed.

'Her name is Nols. They were preparing her for the Giving when Glock and I arrived here,' Jasmine added in a flat voice. 'One of their fishing boats had plucked us, half drowned, from the water. If it had not been for Glock risking his own life by holding me up, I would have perished long before.'

Glock snorted. 'Risking my life?' he jeered. 'Why, I could have held twenty of you, weakling! My talisman protects me from drowning.'

'Indeed!' said Jasmine dryly. 'Will it protect you from The Fear also?'

Glock ran his tongue over his lips and fell silent.

'They cheered when they saw us,' Jasmine went on, looking out at the crowd. 'We thought we were welcome. But they were only rejoicing because Nols is much loved, and they had found strangers to take her place.'

She groaned. 'We tried to scare them into freeing us by saying we were not alone. We had no idea it was *true*! Oh, why did you follow us?'

'What else could we do?' said Lief sharply, to hide the pain in his heart. 'You were rushing headlong into danger—and dragging Glock with you!'

'Glock forced me to bring him!' Jasmine snapped. 'He threatened to have me stopped if I did not.'

'I thought you knew what you were doing,' snarled Glock. 'That was my mistake. I fell into water. My fighting spider, which cost five gold pieces, escaped. And now I am about to be sacrificed to a monster.

'Why did you take this risk, Jasmine?' Lief sighed. '*The Girl With the Golden Hair* told of goblins in the underground, and made clear they were to be feared.'

Jasmine shook her head stubbornly. 'A man called

Doran the Dragonlover came here. He visited at least twice, and for him it was a place of peace and beauty.'

'How can you know this?' Lief demanded.

'I read it in the *Annals*,' Jasmine said. 'After his first visit, Doran wrote a verse about these people. After the second, he changed the verse, to disguise the meaning of what he had written.'

'Why?' asked Barda bluntly.

'Don't you see?' Jasmine exclaimed. 'Doran wanted the secret kept. He thought *we* were a threat to the goblins, not the other way around.'

'Then Doran was a fool,' growled Barda.

'*You must not say that!*'

The companions saw the old woman, Nols, glaring at them through the bars of the cage.

'You must not speak ill of Doran in this place,' she repeated in a lower voice. 'He was a friend to us in ages past. Before The Fear grew.'

'Come away, Grandmother,' muttered Clef, pulling her back.

'They said an evil thing of Doran,' complained Nols. 'I could not let it pass.'

'Doran is only a character of legend,' said Clef impatiently. 'It does not matter what they say of him.'

'Doran was not a legend!' exclaimed Nols. 'Was it not Doran who told us to beware of Longhairs and other creatures from above? Was it not Doran who said that some of them were servants of the Shadow Lord? How else did we know?'

'Doran was real enough. And he was right to warn you,' Jasmine burst out urgently. 'But we are the Shadow Lord's enemies, not his friends.'

The two faces, old and young, turned to look at her in surprise.

'We came here only to find the secret way to the Shadowlands,' Jasmine hurried on. 'Many of our people—our loved ones—have been taken captive by the Shadow Lord. We must reach them, and save them. We must! Before it is too late.' Her voice trembled as she said the last words.

Lief and Barda glanced at her quickly, surprised by the desperation in her voice. Jasmine had always been determined to free the slaves. But this strong feeling seemed far more personal. And why had she said, 'before it is too late'?

The expression on Nols' wrinkled face had changed from anger to something like pity.

'If that is true, your journey was always in vain,' she said, shaking her head sadly. 'The Glimmer is the only gateway to the far seas, and it has been sealed by The Fear.'

Jasmine bowed her head, biting her lip. As she did so, the singing in the background rose to a climax, then died away.

'Clef! Nols!' Worron called harshly. 'Get back! The Giving is about to commence.'

15 - The Bargain

Clef took his grandmother's arm and pulled her gently away. At the same moment, the carved panel behind the cage began to slide silently aside.

Through the gap the prisoners could see a narrow band of shore and a sheet of scarlet water. On the other side of the water the cavern ended in a natural wall of high, sheer rock, gleaming red. And in the rock, directly opposite the cage, yawned the entrance to a cave.

Ropes attached to the top of the cage spanned the water and led directly into the cave. Lief saw, to his horror, that several members of the crowd had taken hold of one of the ropes. The cage lurched and began moving towards the water.

'Stop!' Lief shouted. 'We can help you! Use us not to feed The Fear, but to destroy it!'

The goblins pulling the rope hesitated.

'Do not listen to the Longhair!' roared Worron. 'The ceremony must continue!'

The cage jolted and began to slide again.

'We are warriors!' Lief shouted. 'Together we have defeated many monsters—some of them the servants of the Shadow Lord. Free us, return our weapons, and we will rid you of The Fear forever!'

Again the cage stopped moving. The goblins who had been pulling the rope began arguing in low voices.

'I say we let them try!' called Azan from the middle of the crowd. 'They are Longhairs—tall and strong and skilled in battle. Their weapons are of steel. If they could destroy The Fear—think what it would mean to us!'

'No!' Worron's face was twisted with anger. 'Are you mad? If we free the Longhairs, they will turn on us, and the power is not strong enough to hold them all.'

'We will not harm you—we swear it!' called Barda. He pointed to Lief. 'This is the king of Deltora. The magic belt he wears is proof of it. Did Doran tell you no tales of its power?'

Many in the crowd pressed forward curiously as Lief pulled aside his cloak to show the belt at his waist. Plainly they had indeed heard of the Belt of Deltora.

Worron's eyes narrowed with suspicion as he, too, peered through the bars of the cage.

'It resembles the belt in the tales,' he said slowly. 'But I see no magic in it.'

'Perhaps your feeble eyes are not worthy, goblin!' roared Glock, ignoring Barda's efforts to quiet him.

Lief's heart sank as he saw Worron's face harden and draw away.

'You see?' Worron cried, turning to face the crowd. 'Longhairs lie and cheat as easily as they breathe. Did you hear what that one called me? Does it not remind you that Longhairs killed the traitors who went to seek the sun in ages past, calling them "goblins" to excuse the slaughter?'

Glock's lip curled. 'If you are not goblins, what are you?' he muttered under his breath.

'We are not liars, Worron!' shouted Jasmine, desperate to undo the damage Glock had done. 'We will keep our word! We have good reason to do so. We need to pass through The Glimmer. We need to reach the other side. And for that we must face The Fear in any case.'

'I believe she is speaking the truth,' quavered Nols. As heads turned in her direction, she lifted her chin and continued more loudly. 'Whatever you say, Worron, we cannot turn our backs on the chance to rid ourselves of the Fear. Such a chance may never come again.'

'And if the Longhairs betray us?' sneered Worron. 'If they run, steal boats, and take to the seas? What of The Giving? We have already had the final warning.'

Nols looked at him proudly. 'I was the chosen Gift before the strangers came here. If they fail us, I will take their place in the cage.'

'If Nols is willing to trust them, then so am I!' called a high-pitched voice in the crowd. Many other voices shouted agreement.

But Worron shook his head, frowning. 'The Fear cannot be destroyed,' he said, folding his hands. 'The sacrifice it demands is hard, but suffering is the way of the world. And if The Glimmer is sealed, so much the better. We have no wish to know those who live on the other side.'

'Now we come to it!' shouted Clef passionately. 'A hundred deaths or one, it is all the same to you, Worron. As long as nothing changes!'

He ran to the cage and began opening the lock.

'Stop!' Worron shouted in rage. He raised his hand. There was a flash, the light dimmed, and Clef was struck motionless.

There was a moment's tense silence. Then Nols walked slowly to her grandson's side.

'Free him, Worron,' she said quietly. 'Or we will take back the power we gave you.'

Worron bared his teeth. 'You cannot—'

'We can,' said Nols. 'We can, and we will.'

Struck dumb with fury, Worron's eyes raked the crowd. He saw no sign of support there. Instead he saw anger, determination, and—hope.

Sulkily he raised his hand again. The light returned to normal. Clef stumbled slightly, shook himself, and without a word began fumbling once more with the lock on the door of the cage.

In moments the door was open. One by one Lief, Barda, Jasmine and Glock hobbled to freedom. They stretched their arms and legs in relief as Clef and Azan cut their bonds. Others in the crowd brought their weapons.

'Now we will see,' sneered Worron, standing well back.

'I think I will warm my sword on him before we go,' Glock muttered, flexing his cramped hands.

'Save your sword for the beast!' snapped Jasmine. She measured the distance to the cave with her eyes. 'How best should we reach it?'

'I have a plan,' Lief began. 'The cage—'

'I know what you are thinking, and I agree,' Barda interrupted. 'But you are no part of this, Lief. You must go to high ground, and wait.'

Lief shook his head. 'I cannot do that. I will not.' The thought of Marilen waiting anxiously at home flashed into his mind, but he thrust it away.

'Do what Barda says, Lief,' said Jasmine. 'You have no choice.'

'You will go to high ground or be carried there,' growled Glock. 'You must be protected.'

'It is too late for that!' Lief exclaimed. 'No-one here is safe now. If we fail to kill The Fear, it will destroy the village. And there is no way out of this cavern.'

Clef, Nols and Azan had been watching them anxiously. Now they came closer. 'Please delay no further,' muttered Clef. 'The Fear will any moment grow tired of waiting.'

Still the companions hesitated, Lief glaring defiantly at the rest.

Kree screeched and flapped his wings. Jasmine looked up, alert.

'The thing in the cave is stirring,' she murmured.

But the goblins knew it already. They were all shuddering and drawing back. Some of the children had begun to cry.

Lief leaped past Barda and swung himself onto the top of the cage. 'Make haste!' he shouted.

Seeing that he had taken matters out of their hands, Glock, Jasmine and Barda clambered after him.

'Take the ropes!' Lief called to Clef and Azan. 'Pull us over to the cave!'

As Clef and Azan ran to do his bidding, a harsh, grating call sounded over the water. It was low and full of menace. Foam-flecked waves began to surge from the cave. Water splashed against the wall and flooded through the open panel into the cage and beyond.

'You see?' Worron hissed to Clef. 'Your defiance and your grandmother's foolishness will be our death!'

Clef made no reply. Shoulder to shoulder with Azan, he was heaving on the rope. The cage slid down the shore and reached the water. A few in the crowd cheered.

'Our torches are lost, and the cave is dark,' Lief called. 'Can you light it?'

'Worron can,' Clef called back. 'If he is willing. He has all our power in his hands.' He turned his head to where Worron stood scowling furiously. 'Will you light The Glimmer, Worron?' he asked. 'If it is what the people want?'

'No, I will not!' Worron shrieked in a frenzy of rage.

'How dare you ask it of me? You have chosen to go against my orders. You will all die because of your folly. And I will not lift a hand to help you!'

Another fearsome cry sounded from the cave. The crowd retreated in panic. Even Clef and Azan took a stumbling step backwards, and the rope slackened and sagged.

But Nols stood her ground. 'Keep pulling!' she shouted. Clef and Azan gripped the rope and heaved once more. The violently rocking cage with the four companions clinging to its roof was lifted clear of the waves and began moving away from the shore.

Lief looked back. Foam swirled around Nols' ankles as she stared at Worron, her face filled with contempt. Her voice floated clearly across the water.

'Since you were chosen I have followed you loyally, Worron, despite my doubts. But now you show your true colours. You are a tyrant and a coward! You . . .'

'The old crone's tongue is as sharp as yours, weakling,' Glock sniggered to Jasmine.

'Hold your own tongue, Glock, or I will tear it out by the roots!' flashed Jasmine. Satisfied at having stirred her to anger, Glock snorted with laughter and was still.

And so it was that Nols' final words came to their ears loud and clear. Words that hit Lief and Barda like thunderbolts.

'I withdraw my trust in you, Worron,' Nols cried. 'You are not fit to lead the Plumes. You are not fit to be Piper.'

16 - The Fear

Stunned, Lief stared back at the shore and at the crowd gathered there. Suddenly he was seeing the land for what it was—an island.

'The secret sea!' he breathed. 'We found it, and we did not know! And that island, the people—'

'Goblins,' growled Glock.

'No!' Lief exclaimed hoarsely. 'Pirrans! The descendants of the Pirrans who followed Plume. The owners of the mouthpiece of the Pirran Pipe!'

'I never dreamed the islands could be anywhere but in the open sea,' gasped Barda.

'None of us did,' said Lief. 'Doran disguised his map well, by drawing another, of the western sea, beneath it. Yet, if we had thought carefully about the story, we might have guessed the truth.'

'What are you talking about?' Jasmine demanded. 'What truth?' But to her annoyance neither Lief nor Barda seemed to hear her.

'The Pirrans had no time to think,' Lief murmured. 'The Shadow Lord was upon them. They had to hide— disappear from his sight—at once! So they simply commanded the earth to swallow them up. And down below they found another world. A world of which even the Shadow Lord knew nothing.'

Clinging one-handed to the cage, he pulled out his copy of the map and shook it open.

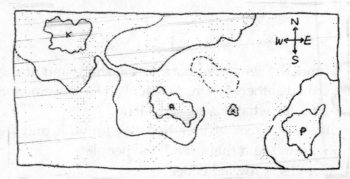

'The lines are not tide-lines,' he said slowly. 'They are cavern walls!'

'And if that is so, we are—here.' Barda pointed mid-way between Plume Island and a gap in the line that ran around the it. 'And that gap is The Glimmer. Though why it has that name I do not know, for it is as black as night.'

Lief stuffed the map back into his pocket. 'If we succeed in this, one piece of the Pirran Pipe will be ours! The Plumes will not be able to refuse us. And the way will be open for the journey to the other islands.'

'I have no idea what you are talking about,' said

Jasmine sharply. 'But I *do* know that if we do *not* succeed in this, we will all be dead.'

She turned to face the cave that yawned before them. The water had stilled, and now lapped peacefully against the rock wall.

'The Fear has heard or felt the approach of the cage,' she said. 'It is quietly waiting for its Gift.'

'Then it is about to get a shock,' said Glock, grinning savagely and drawing his heavy sword.

'It could be *we* who are shocked,' said Jasmine.

Glock puffed out his chest. 'This beast may terrify those puny goblins, but it will be no match for a Jalis warrior. I will slay it single-handed.'

'We had better make a plan, just in case you need help,' said Jasmine dryly. 'Barda?'

'The Fear expects the Gift to be caged, so will approach without fear,' said Barda. 'We can take it by surprise. Glock, Lief and I have swords, so we will see to the tentacles. While the beast is distracted, you, Jasmine, will attack its body from behind. Agreed?'

Lief and Jasmine glanced at one another and nodded. Glock snorted impatiently.

'The Fear lives underground, so no doubt it hunts by touch, hearing, or even smell, rather than by sight,' said Jasmine. 'But we need to see. We need light.'

Lief glanced over his shoulder to the shore. Nols and Worron were still in argument. The crowd was hesitating, looking nervously towards the cave.

'If Nols fails to convince the people to join her, there

will be no light,' he said. 'We cannot depend upon it.'

The cave gaped before them now. As the cage lurched into its mouth, Lief felt a draught on his face— a chill, sour breath that raised the hairs on the back of his neck.

In moments, the light from outside was just a dull glow. Then there was no light at all. The cage came to rest, settling with a creak into thick, sour-smelling blackness. Shallow water lapped gently against its base.

It was very still, very quiet, very dark. And in the darkness, something stirred.

'Ready,' whispered Barda.

Lief held his breath. His sword hand was slippery with sweat.

There was a slithering sound, like the sound of a great snake coiling over rock. And a delicate rippling, like a giant eel writhing through water.

But the sounds seemed to be coming from all around them. They were echoing from the cavern walls and roof, echoing from every direction, so it was impossible to tell where they had begun. The darkness was alive with slithering and splashing.

The companions turned one way, then the other, jostling each other in their confusion.

'Where *is* the thing?' hissed Glock. 'Curse this dark!'

The cage jolted as something prodded the bars on one side.

'There!' Barda whispered. But almost immediately there was a second jolt, this time from the other side.

'It moves swiftly,' Glock growled. 'We will have to separate. I will—'

'No!' Jasmine's voice was very quiet. But something in her flat, even tone sent a cold trickle of fear down Lief's spine. He heard her take a deep breath.

'I think—' she began.

But she never finished what she had been about to say, for at that moment red light began to gleam from the cavern walls. And as the light grew brighter, the companions saw The Fear.

Lief heard Glock cursing under his breath, saw Jasmine's eyes darken, felt Barda's body stiffen, fought his own terror.

The Fear was not on one side of the cage or the other. It was not above them, or below them.

It was everywhere.

Gigantic tentacles like the twisting trunks of vast trees filled the cavern from wall to wall, from floor to roof. The cage suddenly seemed tiny—dwarfed by the great mottled coils that wound above and around it.

At the end of every tentacle wriggled bundles of slimy white threads tipped with vicious hooks. Some of these were already sliding delicately through the bars of the cage. Others were slithering like worms over the dripping cavern walls as the tentacles from which they grew writhed into position.

And on the far wall of the cavern, visible only in glimpses as the tentacles moved, was the heart of the horror. A bloated mountain of slimy, billowing flesh hulked there, overflowing from a shell so ancient, so thick and crusted, that it seemed part of the rock itself.

The creature's tiny eyes were invisible. Its hideous hooked beak gaped greedily as its tentacles explored its domain. Perhaps it had already realised that the cage was empty. But it could sense that prey was near.

It was in no hurry. It knew there was no escape.

'The plan!' muttered Glock. 'What are we to—'

Lief felt an insane urge to laugh. Plan? The plan was a joke. The plan had been based on knowledge that was so out of date as to be worse than ignorance.

That carving on the panel—how long ago had it been made? Two hundred years? Five hundred? More?

Why had they not expected this? For centuries, The Fear had been left unchallenged. It had been unseen, even by its victims. It had been known only by its terrible cries, and the waves with which it flooded the land.

And in the darkness, it had grown.

Lief became aware that Glock had crawled to his feet, and was lumbering towards the nearest coiled tentacle, his sword raised high above his head.

'Glock! No—' roared Barda.

But he was too late. With a savage shout, Glock brought the sword down with all his strength. The mighty blade struck the tentacle with the sound of an axe on stone—and snapped in two.

17 - Nightmare

Glock stared, stunned, at his broken sword. He seemed unable to believe what had happened. He did not react to the rasping growl that echoed around the cavern. He did not move as the bruised tentacle shifted.

'Glock! Beware!' Jasmine screamed.

The tip of the tentacle lashed upward, striking like a snake. Slimy white threads caught Glock around the neck, the hooks burying themselves deep in his flesh. He fell to his knees, screaming in agony. In an instant the tentacle had whipped around his body, and he was being lifted into the air.

Jasmine darted forward.

'No, Jasmine!' shouted Lief.

But Jasmine either did not, or would not, hear. With Kree shrieking above her head, she leaped to the rising tentacle as once she had leaped from tree to tree in the Forests of Silence. She clung motionless for a moment, then, thrusting her dagger between her teeth. she began to climb, her fingers digging into the hard, slimy surface.

'Your dagger will be useless against it, Jasmine!' cried Barda. 'Glock is lost. Save yourself!'

But Jasmine had already reached Glock's limp body and was climbing over it, to the tentacle's tip. The tip was bent, the white threads stretched taut as they kept their strangling, stinging hold around the groaning man's neck.

Jasmine snatched her dagger from her mouth and slashed at the roots of the white threads. One by one the threads fell away, thick, green liquid bubbling from the ragged wounds.

The Fear bellowed in rage. The injured tentacle writhed. Its grip on Glock loosened and he fell like a stone. Jasmine jumped after him, shouting to Kree.

Rigid with horror, Barda and Lief looked down. They caught sight of Jasmine's dark head break clear of the water, saw her stagger upright among the heaving mottled coils of the beast. She was dragging Glock by the shoulders, holding his head out of the water.

Shrieking, Kree swooped at the tip of the injured tentacle, stabbing at it, darting aside as it lunged for him. He could not hope to save Jasmine. All he could do was try to distract the beast, and give her time to save herself.

Did Glock still live? Lief could not tell. But his heart seemed to rise to his throat as he saw a jagged slash of silver in the churning water.

Glock's huge hand still gripped his sword as

though, alive or dead, he would never let it go.

The Fear's terrible, ear-splitting roars echoed around the cavern. It thrashed the water, and Glock and Jasmine disappeared in a whirlpool of foam. Great waves swelled and rushed towards the cavern entrance, and into Lief's mind flashed a picture of the Plumes waiting on the shore.

The tentacles around the cage tightened and the bars cracked like twigs. The tentacles above Lief and Barda began uncoiling and writhing downwards, their pale undersides ribbed like the belly of a snake.

The light flickered, and went out.

'Jump!' Barda roared.

Lief leaped for his life as the cage collapsed beneath him. He hit the foaming water and went under. He tumbled helplessly in the deathly chill, his mouth and nose filled with the taste and smell of the beast. Splinters from the shattered cage and the bones of long-dead victims of The Fear swirled with him in the stinking froth.

His right shoulder slammed against something solid, and agonising pain jolted down his arm. Blindly he reached out with the other hand, felt rock under his fingers and managed to haul himself to his feet.

He had been swept against the cavern wall. Shivering and panting, water foaming to his waist, he clung to the rock. His eyes were tightly closed, but slowly he became aware of wavering light against his eyelids. Somehow, as waves pounded their island, a little band of Plumes had managed to summon up their power once more.

Lief forced his stinging eyes open and, through a flickering red haze, saw a scene of nightmare.

Vast, thrashing tentacles filled the cavern. The water heaved and boiled with their writhing. One of the tentacles, the one Jasmine had attacked, twisted more wildly than the rest, its blunted tip jerking horribly, spattering the walls and roof with thick blobs of slimy green.

Lief shrank back, and only then realised that he was clutching a thick rock shelf that jutted from the cavern wall at water level.

Slowly, painfully, he hauled himself onto the ledge. He crawled to his feet, flattened himself against the rock and began searching desperately for some sign of Jasmine, Barda or Kree.

But he could see nothing. Nothing but the coiling tentacles, quietening now, beginning to search more patiently, more thoroughly. The threads at the tips of the nine uninjured arms wriggled, stretched and pulsed like hideous worms as they probed the rocky walls, combed the dark red water. Seeking, seeking . . .

How many crushed, drowned bodies were drifting just below that scum-covered surface, waiting to be found? Was Glock there? Barda? Jasmine?

Lief closed his eyes, fighting down the despair that threatened to engulf him. He tried to block everything from his mind but the need to survive. Cautiously, wincing with pain, he moved his injured arm.

Only then did he realise that his hand was not only numb, but empty. His sword was gone.

Forcing down panic, he made himself think. He was certain that he had been gripping the sword when he hit the water. He could remember the feel of the hilt in his hand as he was being tumbled about in the foam.

But then he had crashed against the rock—against the rock ledge on which he was standing now. He peered into the dark, foam-flecked water lapping at his feet. His stomach lurched as he saw the long, slow turn of pale, ribbed flesh.

One of the beast's tentacles was writhing just below the ledge. If he had still been standing there . . .

The tip of the tentacle broke the water's surface. Lief watched in fascinated dread as the worm-like fingers stretched towards the ledge, touched it, and began to ooze forward.

He stood rigidly still, hardly daring to breathe. If he tried to edge away, the fingers would sense movement and lash out, as they had lashed out at Glock. But if he stayed where he was, the fingers would soon reach his feet. Then they would creep up to his ankles. And as soon as they felt warm flesh . . .

'Be very still.'

The voice was just a breath. Stiffly, Lief turned his head to the right and saw Barda edging out of a shallow hole in the cavern wall, only an arm's length away.

Barda was dripping and bedraggled. His face was

smeared with blood, and blood matted his sodden hair. But his sword gleamed as he raised it high.

Lief looked down again. The toes of his boots were covered in a mass of squirming, hooked threads. Cold sweat broke out on his brow. His stomach churned with revulsion.

The threads oozed forward. The tentacle tip from which they grew rose higher from the water, nodding horribly . . .

'Go!' roared Barda, and struck, his blade slicing cleanly through the white threads, a hair's breadth from their roots.

Slipping and sliding on the uneven footholds in the wall, Lief scrambled aside. The water beneath the ledge began to heave and bubble as though it were boiling.

'Get behind the shell!' he heard Barda shouting.

Lief glanced over his shoulder. Huge coils of the injured tentacle were heaving upward, bursting out of the water in cascades of spray. The jerking, blunted tip, oozing slime, was dashing itself against the ledge where he had been standing.

Barda was hurriedly squeezing back into his shallow hiding place. But he would not be safe there for long. Nowhere would be safe for long.

The beast was screeching ferociously, its tentacles pounding the water once more. The light began to flicker. A wave crashed into Lief, throwing him to his knees, jarring his injured arm which throbbed agonisingly. Gasping, he crawled on, half in and half out of the water.

He could not move back. He could not stay where he was. His only choice was to move on.

For long, agonising minutes he crawled, expecting every moment to be snatched into the air. But at last he realised that the water beside him was calming. The rock shelf had broadened. Bleached, white bones lay in heaps all around him. He dared to look up.

He had reached the end of the cavern, the heart of The Fear.

Now he could clearly see what lay behind the huge mass of tentacles. He could see the cruel, tearing beak He could even see the small, pale eyes staring vacantly ahead. He could see the shapeless body and the vast, stone-like shell which rose halfway to the cavern roof, dull blue, ridged with the growth of centuries.

The shell had become part of the cavern wall. The Fear could not move. But it did not need to. Its mighty arms were more than long enough to reach every corner of its domain. No prey could escape it.

A small movement on the shell caught Lief's eye. He stared, and almost cried out.

For the movement was Jasmine! Jasmine was crawling up the stony blue ridges, dagger in hand.

As if Jasmine felt Lief's gaze she looked down. Their eyes met, and her face broke into a broad smile.

Perhaps she saw Lief's joy at seeing her alive. Perhaps she felt joy of her own. But she did not speak. She simply pointed downwards, lifted her hand to Lief, palm outwards, and climbed on.

His heart beating wildly, Lief looked to where she had pointed. He saw Glock slumped against the shell, his broken sword still clutched in his hand.

Glock was breathing in shallow, painful gasps. Great, swollen wounds burned scarlet on his neck and face. Kree was standing motionless beside him, as though on guard.

By the time Lief looked up again, Jasmine had reached the top of the shell. As Lief watched in terror, she jumped lightly onto the billowing flesh that spilled from it, lay face down and began to wriggle forwards.

The Fear's tiny eyes showed no sign that it felt her. Perhaps it did not. Or perhaps it thought no more of Jasmine than a human would think of a crawling fly.

Half sliding, half crawling, Jasmine moved on until she was just behind the beast's eyes. Deliberately she raised her dagger. Lief stood, paralysed, helpless, unable to do anything but watch.

His heart leaped as Jasmine thrust the dagger down with all her strength, burying it to its hilt between the creature's eyes. But then, with a thrill of terror, he saw those pale, vacant eyes roll back and fix on Jasmine's face. He saw Jasmine stare, unbelieving, as the dagger sprang back in her hand, rejected by the rubbery flesh it was supposed to pierce.

Then, with a strike so fast that it was like a blur, a tentacle whipped backwards, curled around Jasmine's body and snatched her, screaming, into the air.

18 - Rainbows

A black shape streaked upward. It was Kree, his golden eyes fixed and savage. He did not attempt to attack the vast coil that held Jasmine, but instead swooped fearlessly at the tentacle's tip, stabbing and tearing at the hooked white fingers that wriggled there.

But this time The Fear did not loosen its grip. And more tentacles were curling back, their tips whipping through the air, striking at the darting bird, reaching for Jasmine's dangling feet.

Lief plunged wildly forward, aware of nothing but Jasmine's peril. He seized a bone from the scattered pile on the rock and, left handed, threw it as hard as he could into the squirming maze of tentacles above his head.

The bone hit one of the tentacle tips. The tentacle jerked and recoiled. Shouting savagely, Lief threw another bone, then another.

From the corner of his eye he glimpsed a figure

moving near him on the ground. He could not pause to see who it was. A tentacle was coiling directly towards him. He spun a bone at it, and caught it on the tip. Some of the white threads curled back, jerking and oozing slime.

Lief shouted in triumph. But the sound died on his lips as another tentacle reared up from the churning water in front of him. It lashed at him with such speed that he barely saw it before it had wrapped itself around him. His head spun as he was swung off his feet, struggling and kicking.

The tip of the tentacle which was holding him bobbed beside his shoulder. White stubs waggled there, dripping slime. This was one of the arms that had been injured. But, injured or not, it had him. He could feel its coils tightening around his chest, crushing his ribs, squeezing the life from him.

Struggling for breath, he was swept up into the squirming centre of the tentacle mass. And it was then that he heard a bellowing cry from below.

And saw, in the very midst of the place where the tentacles began, directly in front of the beast's gaping beak, the hulking, swaying figure of Glock.

Glock had crawled from hiding. Crawled, ignoring agony, ignoring fear, into the centre of the terror.

Now, bent and staggering, he raised his shattered sword. 'So you tear us apart, and cast away our bones!' he roared. 'You like your meat soft, do you? Well, see how you fancy this!'

124

And he fell forward, plunging his arm and the jagged stump of his great blade straight down the beast's throat.

A ghastly, bubbling roar echoed through the cavern. The tentacle holding Lief seemed to freeze in the air. Then it began to shudder and jerk. Lief heard Kree screech, felt the coil that held him loosening, felt himself slipping. His fingers scrabbled on the slimy, ridged skin of the tentacle's underside as he plunged down into the water.

He rose to the surface spluttering and swung around, frantically trying to see Jasmine among the foam and the twisting coils of the beast.

'Lief! Here! Make haste!'

Barda was splashing towards him. Barda was seizing him by the waist and hauling him recklessly over the squirming tentacles towards the rock.

Lief struggled weakly. 'Jasmine!' he choked.

'She is safe! There, see? By the shell!' Barda shouted.

Lief twisted his neck, blinking through a haze of water. He saw Jasmine kneeling by the heaving body of the beast.

Jasmine's hair was streaming with water and blood. But she was alive. Alive!

Filli was clasped in her arms. Kree was on her shoulder. As Lief watched, she raised her head, looked straight at him, and then up, above his and Barda's heads.

Her face changed. She stumbled to her feet.

'Lief!' she shrieked. Lief himself looked up and suddenly understood.

Above his head great tentacles were curling inward. And they were swaying, like great trees about to fall.

To fall!

Lief twisted free of Barda's clasp and began clawing his own way through the water, heedless of the pain in his arm. Together he and Barda struggled forward. Together they reached the rock, sprawled to safety, just as the giant tentacles began crashing down, carving great furrows in the water. Water shot to the roof and rained down again, pounding on the rock, beating on the quivering, dying body of The Fear.

And then, quite suddenly, it was over, and there was silence.

Lief, Barda and Jasmine crawled to their feet. Nothing moved in the cavern but the water lapping against the rock. Red light flickered feebly. The tentacles, already paling to shades of grey, lay half-submerged, like the trunks of vast, drowned trees.

And Glock lay still, crushed beneath the mass of mottled flesh at the heart of the Fear. Only his head and shoulders were free. His eyes were closed.

They clambered over to him, and knelt by his side.

'Glock,' said Lief softly.

Glock's eyes opened. They were glazed, but a small spark burned deep within them.

'It is dead, then?' he asked.

'Yes,' said Barda quietly. 'You defeated it, Glock.

Single-handed. As you always said you would.'

Glock nodded slowly. 'That is good,' he said. 'I thought—there is one place where the beast is not protected. One place. If only I can reach it. If only . . .'

The light in the cavern was slowly brightening. The jewel-like colour fell on Glock's face. 'I am dying,' he murmured, almost in wonder. 'But that is good also. For what use is a Jalis without his sword arm?'

'You will fight again, Glock,' said Lief.

Glock's mouth twisted into a mocking smile. 'Not in this life,' he said. His eyes shifted to Jasmine's face. 'The girl knows. She does not lie to me, or to herself. She knows I am finished.'

Jasmine met his gaze. Her eyes were burning with unshed tears, but she moved her head slightly in a nod.

'I have called you weakling more than once, girl. But that—was sport,' the dying man said huskily. 'You have the heart of a Jalis. Take my talisman from my neck. It is yours now. May it serve you well.'

Jasmine's eyes widened, but she did not stir.

A flicker of impatience crossed Glock's face. 'Take it!' he muttered. 'Take it now, so I may see it in your hands. '

Jasmine reached forward and did as she was told.

Glock stared at the small, faded bag, and again his mouth twisted into a smile. 'You may think that it did not serve *me* so well,' he said. 'But remember this. The dearest wish of a Jalis is to die fighting in a great cause. And that I have done.'

The light in the cavern grew brighter, brighter, and suddenly it seemed to Lief that rainbows began to dance within it. Blinking, dazzled, he looked up.

His eyes had not been deceiving him. Visible at last, on the other side of the slowly collapsing body of The Fear, was the mouth of a tunnel. And from the tunnel streamed rainbow light that mingled with the cavern's scarlet so that it seemed that the very air was shining.

'The Glimmer,' Jasmine whispered.

A faint sound reached their ears. The sound of the Plumes cheering wildly on the shore. They had seen the light.

'Lief.' Glock's voice was very low. Lief bent over him.

Rainbows played on Glock's ravaged face. 'The way to the Shadowlands is open,' he murmured. 'Now—you can find my people. You can bring them home.'

Lief nodded. His heart was so full that he was unable to speak.

'When you find them,' the dying man said, 'I would like you to—tell them of me.'

Lief found his voice. 'I will tell them, Glock,' he said. 'I swear it.'

Glock nodded slightly with satisfaction. Then his eyes closed, and he spoke no more.

19 - The Hand of Fate

The island had been battered mercilessly by The Fear's rage. But the Plumes were singing as their boats carried Lief, Barda, Jasmine and Glock to the shore, skimming over the water like brown leaves swept by the wind.

And as the boats landed, the song rose in joy until it seemed to fill the vast cavern. The words echoed from the glowing walls, rolling in waves of beauty over the scarlet sea.

> *Above our land the tumult rages*
> *Struggle echoes through the ages*
> *There the strife may never cease*
> *But here below we dwell in peace.*
> *Where timeless tides swamp memory,*
> *Our sunless prison makes us free.*
> *The gem-glow lights our rocky walls,*
> *And dragons guard our shining halls.*

'It is not a song of death, but of life,' said Jasmine softly as the last, pure notes drifted on the air. 'I knew it was so.'

Lief and Barda glanced at her curiously, but did not question her. Her eyes were fixed on the boat which Nols herself had guided—the boat in which Glock's body lay, shrouded in scarlet.

'So Glock will remain here,' Jasmine sighed. 'It seems strange . . .'

'Your friend will be honoured among us,' said Nols, stepping forward and putting her small hand on Jasmine's arm. 'He will lie with the Pipers of Plume, and never be forgotten.'

Jasmine thought for a moment, then smiled slightly. 'Glock would like that,' she said. 'He would like to take his place with chiefs.'

Nols bowed. 'Our debt to him, and to you, can never be repaid. We have little enough to give, but whatever we have is yours. Boats for your journey. Food. Light, as far as we are able to supply it . . .' She paused, waiting.

Lief took a deep breath. This was the opportunity he had been hoping for, but now that it had come he almost feared to take it.

'There is one thing which only you can give us,' he said slowly. 'It is a treasure we dearly need—though only for a time. The mouthpiece of the Pirran Pipe.'

Nols stepped back, a stricken look on her face. The people behind her murmured and whispered.

Dismayed, Lief glanced quickly at Barda and

Jasmine. Barda was frowning in angry disbelief. Jasmine, who still knew nothing of the Pirran Pipe, was simply confused.

'I know we ask a great deal,' Lief said, keeping his voice steady with difficulty. 'But I beg you to consider our request. If we are to save our people from the Shadow Lord we must make the Pipe whole again. It is the one thing the Shadow Lord fears. The one thing that may give us time to—'

Nols held up her hand to stop him. 'You do not understand,' she said, her voice trembling. 'It is not that we *will* not give you the mouthpiece of the Pipe. It is that we *cannot*. It was lost long ago.'

It was like a blow to the pit of Lief's stomach. He stared at Nols, unable to speak.

'Not lost—stolen!' said Worron's sharp voice. He stepped forward, still an imposing figure in the long red robe and scarlet headpiece he had not yet put aside. 'The symbol of the Piper's leadership was stolen from the people by the Seven Traitors—the wicked ones who left the safety of our seas for the world above.'

'It was in ancient times, when the Plumes' time in the world below the world had not been long,' said Nols, more quietly. 'The people of those days were not accustomed to the caverns, as we are. It is written that the rebels planned to find a place of safety, then return and lead the Plumes back into the sun. But they never returned'

She sighed. 'Doran the Dragonlover told our

ancestors that they had all lost their lives. He knew a tale of it. It was an old tale often told, he said, by the members of a savage Longhair tribe called Jalis, whose own ancestors had done the killing.'

'Yes.' Worron's eyes narrowed maliciously. 'The Seven Traitors were destroyed, and the mouthpiece of the Pipe with them, no doubt. So if the Pipe is what you have come here to seek, Longhairs, your journey, your time, and your friend's life, have all been wasted.'

Into Lief's mind came the memory of Glock grinning over a mug of ale. Glock, the last of the Jalis. His eyes suddenly burned with tears, and he looked quickly away.

He saw that Jasmine had taken the little cloth bag from her neck, and was opening it. Plainly she, too, was thinking of Glock.

Lief turned back to Worron. 'It is our loss, certainly, that the three pieces of the Pipe cannot be joined once more,' he said, struggling to keep his voice steady. 'But The Fear is dead, Worron. The Plumes are free of it. So nothing has been wasted.'

'Indeed it has not,' said Clef loudly. 'We—'

He broke off, staring. Lief saw that Nols, too, was staring. And Worron. And all the Plumes crowding behind them.

But they were not staring at him. They were looking at Jasmine—or rather, at the dusty, oddly-shaped piece of wood that Jasmine was holding in the palm of her outstretched hand.

There was a moment's stunned silence. Then Nols reached out and took the wooden object reverently. Slowly she crouched and dipped it into the water. The dust of centuries loosened and lifted away in a fine cloud. And when she stood up once more, the thing in her hands seemed to glow—a small miracle of shining wood and strange, carved patterns.

'The mouthpiece of the Pirran Pipe!' she whispered.

Worron's mouth was opening and closing like the mouth of a fish. 'Where—? Where—?' he stuttered.

'Glock had it all the time,' Jasmine said calmly. 'It was part of the talisman passed down to him by his family. He had no idea it was anything more than a lucky charm. Neither did I, until a few moments ago—and even then I only suspected the truth.'

Wisely, she said no more. She wanted Glock buried in state with the Pipers of Plume. She knew better than to admit how his ancestors had come by the object that the crowd was pressing forward to see.

Nols' face was alight with joy. 'It is a miracle!' she cried. 'Our treasure has been returned to us. Now we can pay our debt to you.'

Lief, looking down at her beaming face and at the joyous faces clustered around her, wondered how he ever could have thought these people were ugly. He wondered, too, at the chance that had brought the mouthpiece of the Pirran Pipe back to its rightful owners.

And, finally, he wondered if it was not chance at all, but something else.

He turned to Barda, who was still staring at the gleaming mouthpiece in amazement. 'We have reached our first goal, Barda,' he murmured. 'And the way is open to our second. According to the map, the island of Auron is next. '

Barda shook his head slowly. 'First we must find our way back to Del. Doom is waiting for us there, with supplies, fighters—'

'No!' cried Jasmine fiercely. 'There can be no delay! Time is running out! We must—'

She broke off as Lief and Barda turned to her.

'Why do you say this, Jasmine?' Barda demanded.

Jasmine wet her lips. 'I heard . . . heard that the Shadow Lord was going to kill the prisoners. Very soon.'

'Birds told you this?' Lief asked sharply.

Jasmine hesitated. It was not in her nature to lie. But she did not want Lief to know that she had entered the sealed room, that she had spoken to the sister he had tried to keep from her.

She knew she could not bear to see the look on his face as he tried to deny, or explain, his deceit and betrayal of trust. She preferred to put it out of her mind. To focus on the task at hand. To lose her thoughts in action.

So she pressed her lips together, and nodded.

'Then we must go on—the three of us,' said Lief instantly.

'No!' Barda growled. 'You, at least, cannot—'

'I can,' said Lief firmly. 'And I think it was always meant that I should.'

'But you are Deltora's king!' cried Jasmine. Lief was saying just what she had wanted him to say. Yet, suddenly, she found herself filled with doubt.

Lief met her anxious gaze squarely. 'I have thought of this long and hard,' he said. 'I am the king, but I am still Lief. I must do what I must do.'

'No!' Barda protested, but Lief shook his head.

'I cannot be a prisoner,' he said. 'That is what happened to the kings and queens of our past, and it was their ruin. It was not what Adin intended when he created the Belt of Deltora. He—'

Feeling a light touch on his arm, he turned to see Nols looking up at him.

'I asked Azan to arrange sleeping quarters for you, on the high ground, where it is still dry,' Nols said. 'Your wounds must be tended, and you must rest. Ah, Azan!' She smiled welcome at the young Plume who was running, panting, towards her. 'Is all well?'

Azan shook his head, his face furrowed with anxiety. 'No! I fear—I fear all is *not* well,' he stammered. 'The only dry sleeping quarters have been overtaken by two hideous monsters, the like of which I have never seen before.'

Nols looked alarmed. Azan looked piteously at Lief, Barda and Jasmine. 'They are fearsome—as large as my head, with huge fangs, eight legs, and red eyes. And they are fighting with one another savagely, as though they will never stop!' '

The companions glanced at one another. 'I think

we are familiar with the beasts,' Barda said reluctantly. 'Leave them to us.'

Azan's face broke into a relieved smile. 'I will take you to the house!' he said eagerly, darting away.

'Ah, what it is to have heroes among us!' beamed Nols.

'Indeed,' said Lief glumly, as he, Barda and Jasmine, with Kree fluttering overhead, trudged after Azan. 'And if we can defeat The Fear, surely we can control Fury and Flash.'

'I would not count on it,' Barda muttered.

Jasmine turned to Lief. 'What were you telling us, when Nols interrupted you?' she asked.

Lief hesitated. He had thought again about what, in his excitement, he had been about to say. 'Whatever it was, it does not matter,' he lied. 'If we three survived the quest to restore the gems to the Belt of Deltora, why should we not survive this?'

'*This* will end in the Shadowlands,' said Barda gravely. 'And all depends on the Pirran Pipe. We have its first part by a miracle. What of the second and third?'

Lief turned to look back at The Glimmer, shining across the scarlet sea. What perils lay beyond that mysterious gateway? That he could not know. But as he looked, he heard again in his mind that clear, sweet music, beckoning him.

'They are waiting for us,' he said simply. 'I know it. All we have to do—is find them.'

DELTORA QUEST

Books by Emily Rodda

DELTORA QUEST 1

The Forests of Silence

The Lake of Tears

City of the Rats

The Shifting Sands

Dread Mountain

The Maze of the Beast

The Valley of the Lost

Return to Del

The Deltora Book of Monsters
by Emily Rodda and
Marc McBride

The Deltora Journal
by Emily Rodda and
Marc McBride

DELTORA QUEST 2

Cavern of the Fear

2. The Isle of Illusi
3. The Shadowland

■ SCHOLASTIC